PROJE

Written by

ISABELLE LECUYER

With the special collaboration of

Stephanie Dion

Copyright © 2022 Isabelle Lecuyer
All rights reserved.

This book is dedicated to our friends who inspired the story. A special thank-you to Jonathan Ly for his continued dedication to the creation of amazing cover art. You have a gift. Truly.

-Isabelle

To my family and friends who had to deal with my big and weird imagination over the years - the same imagination has brought this book to life with the amazing talent of my best friend, and writer of this book.

-Stephanie

Project Zeus

PROLOGUE

I don't want to be here.

Early last May, I found out I would have to move to the south shore of Montreal, a place called Longueuil. I didn't have a choice but to follow my family here. My dad was transferred to Montreal, but he didn't want to live on the island. It's a big story of how they travelled to Longueuil and bought a house here instead of living on the military base again. So that's why we're on the south shore.

My mom says it's a nice place, but I'm too angry at the unfairness of the world to really care about what she thinks. She can't make me feel better about leaving my friends, about leaving my life behind. She told me not long ago I would be fine, and I responded crossly, 'What do *you* know?' She said she knew a lot; that she had left everything behind for my father; she had given up her education, gotten married, followed him across the world, and often left everything she had come to know to start all over again. But I'm not her, and I don't want that kind of life. I want it to stop. I hate moving around, getting attached to people and places only to have my heart broken again.

I look out my bedroom window. All I see is the top of the small trees planted right outside the clear glass. At the end of the yard, there's a pine tree.

Its branches are wavering up and down, as if they're surfing in the wind. I notice the fence. The neighbour is moving around in his yard, but all I can see is the top of his head. I'm watching this outside, but on the inside, there are just memories. I try to remember the first time we had to move, but it's too long ago to recall the details.

I escape my comfort zone and my restless thoughts. It's time to get dressed. It's time to get back to my screwed-up reality. Mom wants me to spend some time outside. She says I'm getting pale. But I think she fears I might get lonely inside by myself. She obviously won't tell me what she really thinks of me. She's got too much on her mind to worry about me. My dad is off at work, leaving my mom to unpack all the boxes, and organize everything. She's helping my older sister unload and put away her stuff first. Earlier, they were fighting. It went something like this:

"Would you let me talk to you?"

"You don't understand me!"

"Stop yelling! I DO understand!"

"I HATE YOU! I HATE BEING HERE! YOU DON'T CARE. YOU'VE NEVER LOVED ME LIKE DANA …"

And when she refers to me, I stop listening. My sister has always thought me the favourite of all three kids, and that I am better loved by my father. I don't understand why she says that. I think she's just as angry as I am about the whole situation. But she's taking it harder than I am. In fact, I think she's not coping very well. Perhaps, it's deeper than I think it is. Perhaps even, it's something more than what she lets us see on the outside. The problem with the way she expresses herself, and the problem with her in general, is her bad temperament. So, when she gets angry or upset, she pushes my parents away emotionally and sometimes even physically. Worst of all, she blames them for everything wrong in her life.

This leads me to wonder if it was indeed their fault she turned out this way: so angry and broken. Was I broken too, but in my own way? I don't want to turn out like that, but I do feel like something has shattered within me. Something I might never be able to get back. I feel vulnerable. I feel like the world is after me, and it will be a long way to happy.

By the time their argument ends with a slammed door, countless curses, and a few silent tears, I've already unpacked and organized the bathroom and the kitchen. Mom slowly enters the kitchen while I'm putting away the last of the plates. Her eyes are red, her cheeks are bright pink, and the vein in her forehead is evident. She's been yelling too much. And she has that look, the one I know too well. The one where you avoid everyone's eyes and pretend like nothing bothers you: she's holding back her pain.

Mom looks around the kitchen for any boxes left to unpack, but they are all empty. She silently moves to the living room and starts unpacking there. I watch her as she pulls the tape off of a rather large box entitled 'living room FRAGILE'. She realizes there's not much she can do but stare at the contents of the box since my dad hasn't set up the wall unit. I know she wants to be left alone, so I quietly move to my room, trying not to think about what she said to me this morning. I don't feel like going outside. I don't feel like meeting anyone.

The truth is, I'm comfortable all alone. Mom doesn't understand that it's harder to make friends when you're sixteen. When you're five, you run to the park, meet someone, and in an hour, you're invited to their birthday party the next weekend. It's not the same anymore. She doesn't want me to stay alone, but all I want *is* to be left alone.

I straighten, and stare at myself in the mirror. My reflection disgusts me. I want to hide away my blond-streaked brown hair with a hat – any hat. Hell, these days, teenagers wear tuques even in the summer. I chose to wear a pair of blue jeans, a printed yellow T-shirt, and running shoes. Simple. Compared to the rest of my life.

* * *

Simple. Like the rest of my life. I've never had to worry about much. Except of course for my own skin and bones. Not even a boyfriend to worry about. Never had one. I'm sixteen years old and never have I, Kassidy Avalon, had a boyfriend. I don't even know if anyone has ever loved me. At least, more than a friend. Is it my hair? Is it too long, or too blond? Is it my intelligence? Is it my horrible sense of humour? It was still unclear in my head. But perhaps this new place would offer me more than the previous ones. Perhaps my dad is the problem. His military status has always intimidated people.

I look around my bedroom and see all the things still left to unpack. I've successfully procrastinated this long to start anything productive now. But my dad is pressuring me to help my mom. Fine … I'll help her first. Then my dad will be on my case about not having finished settling my room. I asked him why it bothered him. He says it's because he has to walk in front of it every day and it's a junkyard. It just bothers him.

Poor excuse if you ask me. Just have to deal with it, until I can get out of here. My escape can wait, though. School is going to start soon, and I still don't know where it is, what my classes are, or anything! Tomorrow, I'll see. I have to find someone to share a locker with. I just hope they won't randomly assign someone. I don't want to end up with some gross guy who doesn't brush his teeth or own a shower. Personal experience.

My mom walks by on her way to her room. I hear her sigh of exasperation when she sees my room. I haven't moved. I'm still sitting on my bed, exercising hard-core procrastination. I know that by tonight, this room will be done the way my mom and dad would like it to be. If it were up to me, I'd keep the junkyard just the way it is. I'll probably end up shoving most of everything in my tiny closet.

My younger sister's room is across from mine. She's already got her bang-bang music on, playing a little too loud. My mom reappears in the hallway with her purse hanging from her shoulder. Although my back is turned, I know she's waiting for me. I can see her reflection in the mirror: her short blond hair, her pale eyes. She changed her sweatpants to a pair of jeans. "Let's go to the store," she says. I smile, grab my sweater, and leave my sister to her noise.

*   *   *

On a late Monday afternoon, the streets are quiet. The heat is exhausting. Perched on the roof of a house, an ominous creature looks down on the street. His neon eyes are locked on a dark-haired girl pulling a load of empty boxes to the driveway. A car's headlights distract her to her left until it turns away. She tugs on the boxes until they reach the curb. She takes a second to scan around her. The houses are all made of brick. The brown brick from across the street bothers her. Most of the other houses are made of softer colors: white, beige, dark brownish red. The young girl turns to look at her mother through the kitchen window. Her mom smiles back at her, one of those 'I'm smiling to hide the pain' sort of smiles.

"Dana Smith," slithers off the tongue of the hidden creature. Its voice is strong. Male. "Confident. Hidden courage. Resilient. Angry. Perfect."

Its eyes glare to the left. A young girl the same age as the previous one is getting out of a car. She is unloading a few, heavy grocery bags.

"Kassidy Avalon," it says. "Shy. Strong heart. Bold. Afraid. Perfect."

It patiently waits for the opportune moment, the precise second. It watches silently, while the wind picks up. The dark grey clouds are forming above. The thunder rumbles across the sky.

Now.

The thunder grumbles louder in the darkening sky. Few seconds separate each lightning strike. The wind blows harder. The creature's coat flaps to the side, revealing six small and bizarre arms. It lifts two of its palms, and points fingers: one at Dana, the other at Kassidy. The lightning bolts shoot down from the sky to strike both girls at the same moment. They collapse to the ground.

Then the creature slowly disintegrates into thin air after a job well done.

DANA

1
THE MEETING

I hear whispers from close by, but I can't tell who it is. There are also loud voices from a place nearby, but I don't recognize them either. There's an irritating buzzing noise from above me, like old school ceiling lights. Everything is dark. I move my head left to right, forcing myself to wake up. I try so hard to pry open my eyes, but it's like my pupils are glued together.

My mom rushes into my decreased sight, followed by a part of my father's face. They look worried and yet relieved. I suppose that's because I'm awake. A woman I've never seen before appears to my right. She reaches into her breast pocket and pulls out a flashlight. Her cold fingers force my eyelids open wider to flare a white light at me.

I wince at the sudden brightness and try to pull away from her.

"Strange," she says. Her voice is soft and warm, compared to the touch of her skin.

"What's wrong?" my mom demands.

No kidding. What's strange? I wonder.

"There's no pupil dilation in Dana's eyes. It's as if your daughter's pupils have changed. They look a little … vertical, instead of round," the doctor explains.

She's obviously crazy, or she just wants to make my parents worry even more. I can tell it's the latter by the look my parents give me. It's as if they're observing me, trying to see what the doctor sees.

I clear my throat. "I see just fine," I say. My voice is rough, as if I hadn't spoken in a few days, or if I had woken up with a bad cold. In fact, my sight is quickly adapting to the light. I see things I've never seen before: details that seem almost irrelevant and yet are extraordinarily vivid right now. I can make out the brown and green in my mom's eyes. I see the split ends in her hair that I normally would never see at this distance, and …

The doctor's skin touches mine again and it feels warmer than the first time. She's checking my pulse with her watch. I hear the ticking of the arrows. My heartbeat is fine.

"Will we be able to take her home tonight?" my father asks. He's in his military uniform. And he looks really tired.

"Oh yes!" the doctor responds. "I had another girl tonight who got hit by lightning. She recovered just fine. We sent her home not too long ago. I'll get the paperwork ready. You'll just have to watch her."

The doctor clears out and leaves my parents and me to ponder on my recovery. It's so strange to have been hit by lightning and walk away from it with no major injuries. But I guess I'm not the only one who can walk away from that.

*   *   *

Last night, I dreamt the most fantastic thing. The wind was cold and harsh, but that barely bothered me. It felt like a warm breeze on my skin, although I was only wearing pyjama pants and a checkered T-shirt. The sky was dark, lit only by the moon and the shining stars. I never paid much attention to them until now. The moon was in all its glory, round and bright. The more I looked at it, the more I saw. I could even make out the crevices and the darker spots. It was all very magnificent until the wind started to pick up. I looked to my left and right. Everything was dark. I looked at my feet. The grand city was shrinking below me! I felt panic at first, but I told myself it was just a dream. And then I realized it wasn't the city that was shrinking, it was me who was flying!

I felt a rush of excitement. My first instincts were to fly around wildly, until I felt a chill caress the back of my neck. It was like my body was telling me that I wasn't alone, that there was someone near me. I scanned around me but saw nothing out of the ordinary. There was just a bird in the distance. A really fast one. In the shape of a human.

I wanted to get a closer look at who it was, but the wind was too strong at this height. I wanted to land, but I didn't know how. I got scared and lost control. The wind sent me plummeting toward the ground.

For a dream, it felt very real. When I woke up, I was sure it *had* been real. I'm surprised I found myself lying in my backyard, wet from the early morning frost. Weren't my parents supposed to be watching me?

My dream was so vivid. It made me sleepwalk for the first time in my life. Then again, I'd never been struck by lightning before. I repeat to myself that it was just a dream, while I stumble inside the house. My back is sore, my arms feel numb, and my legs can barely support my weight. It feels like I had, indeed, fallen from the sky.

Mom is in a deep slumber in a chair by my bed, her head slightly tilted back. She must have dozed off some time during the night. I never even noticed she came in my room to watch over me. I shake her awake.

She blinks open her eyes. She looks confused as she touches her forehead and looks around the room. She slowly comes to realize where she is, and then looks out in the hall. I follow her gaze and see what she's looking for. Dad must have left for work already, because my parents' bedroom door is wide open, and the curtain is drawn to bring the morning light in.

"Are you hungry?" Mom asks me.

I don't know what to answer, but I nod, feeling a pang of pity and sadness for her. Here comes another day where she's abandoned by her husband to carry out all the chores, unpacking, feeding their children, fight with one of them (very likely my sister), and break us apart if we, my siblings and I, start to fight.

Mom gets up and walks to the kitchen. I hear her fumbling in the fridge when I realize what time it is. I stare in disbelief at my alarm clock. It's only 6 am. I lay down on my bed, covering myself to make the shivers stop. My pyjamas are wet from the frost and sticking to my skin. I close my eyes and think of Mom's disappointed eyes upon seeing the empty bedroom. It was more sad than pitiful. I never knew just how lonely she could feel - just like me.

But not exactly like me. She's unhappy and disappointed. I'm angry. Just so angry. And so very tired.

I turn to a more comfortable position. And then it hits me: my father must have seen where I was when he woke up this morning and left for work. If I was sleepwalking, why didn't he bring me back to bed? Did he even see me out there, lying on the grass, right by the driveway?

Today's Tuesday: another day of unpacking and organizing. All I'm thinking about is my dream from last night. Why did it feel so real? I still feel the wind tickling my skin and whipping at my hair. I still see the person flying toward me, as clearly as I see the boxes around my bed.

"Dana?"

I look to the door. My mom is standing in the doorframe dressed in jeans, a pink polo shirt, and running shoes. She tied her thin brown hair in a ponytail. She looks as though she's going golfing. In all my wondering, I didn't notice that Mom made breakfast, woke up my brother, got dressed, and was now checking-in on me.

"What are you still doing in bed?" she asks me. She walks in the room and heads for the curtains.

"Recovering. I had a bad night," I respond. I prepare for the sunlight to hit my face and burn my eyes. But it doesn't come. My mom carefully reaches under the curtain and opens the window.

"We have to go to your school today. You have to register for your classes," she tells me while stealing a look around my bedroom. It's a mess. I had prioritized helping her instead of making my personal space habitable.

"Okay," I answer. But my interest at the moment is only the dream. I wanted to be left alone to think about the details of the dream before they started to fade from my memory. But the only way that would happen is if the world stopped spinning. So far, I wasn't able to do anything I wanted to do. I'm forced to do things that are of no interest to me, like starting a new life.

"We're leaving in fifteen," Mom informs me, just as she's about to leave the room. "We're biking there." She closes the door. From down the hall, she adds, "And Cole is coming!"

"Urf," I whisper to myself, but I really mean to say worse words.

My twelve-year-old brother is the annoying type who seeks attention whenever possible. He has the habit of opening the door to my room when I'm changing, eating his stupid marshmallows on my bed and dropping them all over the place (because, of course, they have to be the tiny ones).

I get up from the comfort of my bed and slowly pick out my clothes. Am I supposed to look nice? Am I to make an impression? Was there going to be a lot of people there?

Just as I'm about to pull off my shirt, the door flies open. Cole charges in and plunks down on the bed.

"Get out," I snarl. He just stares back with his innocent, brown eyes. I notice his brown hair is thick and getting too long. The thought alone that he was going to be an embarrassment made his presence all the more irritable.

It was over thirty degrees out and he's wearing a pair of grey sweatpants and its matching long sleeve sweatshirt. He's going to boil if we're biking all the way to my new school. Pff ... not my problem. Or maybe it will become my problem when he complains all the way there, and he is sweating balls while we're waiting in line with all these other teenagers staring at us.

"Cole, get out!"

I glare at him. I can't stand him.

Cole has always craved attention, and he will do anything to get it. Since the move, Cole has had a lot of trouble making friends (since he hardly went outside). He's still at the age where he can just go outside, make friends at the park, and voila. Friendships established. But no. Instead, he decides he wants his sisters' attention instead. I used to have patience enough to handle him every other time we moved. Not anymore. And our sister certainly has no space to take in anything else but herself. That makes Cole even more determined.

I hear my mom's footsteps down the hall, and I call out for her. All she does to help me is shout out his name. Obviously, he just sits there and giggles. "Mom!" I cry again. This time, she appears at the doorway and orders my brother to leave the room. He gets up and leaves as slowly as possible just to piss me off. When the last centimetre of his feet crosses the threshold, I close my door and lock it behind him.

I sigh. My day is off to a bad start. I'm already exhausted and my head is pounding. To make matters worse, my sister downstairs is awake. Her music is obnoxiously loud. Sometimes I wonder if she's deaf, or if her goal is to make the rest of the world disappear.

I pull on a pair of three-quarter sweatpants and a light blue tank top. I imitate my mom and neatly brush my hair into a ponytail. I guess there's no ignoring it – gotta be ready to meet my future.

* * *

Cole is talking to me about hockey. But I couldn't care less. I've no interest in sports or anything my brother's doing. I pretend to listen while looking around me. There are people my age everywhere. There are probably a hundred of them, gathered around a single entrance. At first, I think I'm the only one with my family with me. But I'm not. There's a guy in front of me. He's with his father. They're both tall, tanned, and share the same military look as my father. I can't quite see their faces, but the father and son seem quite alike: same haircut, same body structure, and same stature.

While I scan around, I see a girl standing by herself by the brick wall. She's apart from everyone else, watching us and probably listening to my brother talking. When she notices I'm looking at her, she blushes and looks at her feet. I want to go talk to her, but something holds me back. Perhaps I'm nervous, or perhaps I'm scared. Either way, I'm definitely shy. I don't want to be, but my feet glued to this spot is my biggest hint. The sweaty palms might just be from biking twenty-five minutes. The jitters in my gut might just be from the curiously light breakfast that bounced around when I was hitting each crack and bump on the way here. Or I'm glued here because I'm afraid of talking to other people. Most of all, I'm afraid that I'm going to have to talk to other people – at least, at some point.

To my left, there's a boy about my height. His back is turned to me. All I see of him is his dark hair. It looks as though his head is disproportionate to his body from the back. Perhaps my eyes are seeing it bigger than it really is. He's wearing Nike blue shorts and a beige fishnet muscle shirt. It doesn't look very good. He's talking about his trip to Cuba, as I understand it. And he's looking for someone to give them a very expensive gift. What a show-off.

"Are you listening to me?" Mom asks.

"Sorry. What?"

I jump out of my thoughts to hear my mother quietly scolding me for not listening. I silently thank her prudence and intelligence not to do it so loud in front of everyone. She could ruin my last year of high school forever.

The doors open and the students start filing inside. I've no idea what to expect once inside those doors. This will be my home for the next year. I'll get up every morning to come here and stay here until mid-afternoon. If only there were other ways to spend my time.

While we shuffle forward, still waiting to get inside, I look for the girl that was all alone. Her long blond hair and familiar face prick at the memories of my childhood. I just can't quite put my finger on it, but I feel like I've seen her before. It's highly unlikely, but there was something about her. Before I have the chance to ask my mom, I find her. She's right behind us. She saw I was gazing around. And I must have looked stupid.

"Hi," she quickly says to me as our eyes meet. She smiles. It's an awkward smile, almost like she was forcing it. Her blue eyes are fixed on me. She's taller than me, possibly by a few inches. Her skin is pale, from her face to her thighs and legs, visible only because of her jean shorts. Even her arms are almost colourless.

"Hi," I answer, reaching for her hand. The gesture was intuitive. My body was reacting before my mind had time to process. Who shakes hands anymore, anyway?

My mom, confused, looks behind her at where the voice came from. She steps out of the way so that there is a clear path between the girl and me. A part of me wishes she didn't move, but the other part says that this is best. I should meet someone, whoever it might be. I think it, but really, my entire body is shaking to the bone. I'm terrified of what I'm doing, even as I'm doing it. I try my best to hide it, trying to gain control of the shaking in one limb at a time.

"I'm Kassidy Avalon," she says and gives me her hand in greeting.

"Dana Smith," I reply. I look into my mother's eyes. She seems to be edging me forward to make conversation, but I have nothing to say. I'm quiet for the most part, and that is how I usually am.

"Have you been here long?" she asks. Apparently, she's better at small talk than I am.

"No. I just moved here from Winnipeg. Are you new here too?" I ask her, not at all interested in her answer. I feel stressed and disoriented by the crowd. So many things are happening around me that her answer is irrelevant.

"Yes. I came here from Borden," Kassidy says.

Interestingly enough, her father is in the military too. She says she had to move around a lot because of that, and this is the last place where her parents wanted to settle. It felt like my whole life story. My mom keeps the conversation going and tells Kassidy about our family and where we live.

"Are you serious?" Kassidy says. "Wow! We have so much in common!" she exclaims. "And we live really close to one another. My street is connected to yours."

She seems happy I live close by, and that I have the same kind of background as her. I don't find anything special in those facts, but she does. I pretend to be happy too. I smile. But deep down inside me, I feel uncomfortable and nervous – because now the line is moving and we're getting closer to the sign-up table, my mom is making conversation with a total stranger, sharing our whole lives with her, probably making friends for me, my brother is now fooling around, and I'm suddenly overpowered by the thought that I might forget my name and my date of birth.

"Since there's no one else I know, do you want to share a locker with me? I know they let us have the choice," Kassidy says.

"Yeah," I answer right away. "Sure thing." A weight is gently lifted off my shoulders.

When we step through the threshold, my eyes adjust quicker than usual to the brightness of the artificial lights compared to the sunlight. It's as if there's no difference at all. We stand in front of a table where two older women are sitting. I'm so distracted by everything happening that I barely notice how Cole is running down each hallway in sight. He yells for Mom's attention. He's embarrassing me beyond belief. The weight is added to my shoulders as soon as it had left me. My heart is beating harshly in my chest, and I'm not sure if I should be trying to cower in a corner, dying of embarrassment, if I should focus on my registration, if I should let Kassidy go ahead of me so that I could watch and repeat what she does, or if I should let all these thoughts dizzy me into a panicked surrender.

"Your name," one of them calls.

"Dana Smith," I reply, swallowing my anxiety.

The woman finds my name on a checklist and hands me a bag. She points to where all the other students are headed. I wait for Kassidy to give her name and receive the same pointing finger. There's a long hall before us. It's barely lit, but enough to follow the crowd of young students.

My mom and brother lead us forward while I look around at the details of the school. I guess my mom finally got Cole to stop running around – might be in trouble later. At least, I'll have some peace of mind when we get home. The interior brick walls are painted plain white with no drawings or graffiti on them. There's no proof that this is a high school, until we reach the main hall: it is decorated with photographs of headmasters, teachers, and graduates. There are posters for Kid's Help Line, how to finish a paper, and activities scheduled at the start of term.

I look in the bag I'm holding, and find only irrelevant papers about the school, a plan of the school and other general information. I already know this is a waste of paper, and they will all end up in the same place. Why do they even bother? So, I throw out the bag in the nearest recycle bin. Mom looks at me as though I should have kept the bag. I shake my head and tell her there was nothing of interest in the bag. There was just a bunch of useless papers.

We head up the staircase to the senior hall. Sitting behind a table are two students. Kassidy steps forward and gives our two names. I figure this is where we're given our locker number. The lockers are painted in a pattern of different shades of blue. In the middle of the hall are long beige tables. Some students are sitting together, chatting, and laughing.

"Our locker is here," Kassidy tells me, while leading me to the side. We are the third locker furthest away from the classrooms, the common area, but at least, we have a bench in front. Mom walks past me and sets a few books in the locker that Kassidy opened for her. I'm confused as to why we're already given books before our classes, but most of all, where my mom got my books. This is a whole new system I will have to get used to. For now, all I see are the negative things about this school, this system, these people, and this city. The school is ugly, it looks like a prison, and they waste so much paper. The system chooses your classes for you, and they last all year instead of only a semester at a time. And this city is the largest population of smokers I've ever seen, full of people who don't care about their lives or other peoples' – and that includes its high school population. There is nothing I want more but to be angry at the world.

"So, I'll see you tomorrow, then?" Kassidy asks. "My mom is picking me up, so I have to go."

"No problem. And yes, I suppose we'll see each other tomorrow," I respond. I'm clearly uninformed that school starts *tomorrow*.

Kassidy waves goodbye and disappears around the corner. My mom asks if I want to take a look around before we head home. I prefer to just go home. I'll have all year to look around. She nods in comprehension and leads Cole and I back to where we left our bikes. At this point, all I can think is the end of school when a sudden surge of regret floods me – maybe I should have checked my schedule and located my first class.

*   *   *

The dream disappears from my mind over time, although the feeling of flying still feels real to me. Over dinner, I'm quiet. I think mostly about my classes the next day and where I'm supposed to take the bus. I feel so uninformed and that it makes me really nervous. The first day of school shouldn't be such a stressful thing. But it always is. At every new school, every first day, it's always the same. The same fear, the same anxiety, the same torrent of emotions that twist my mind into a whirlwind of unintelligible thoughts.

My mom tells my dad about Kassidy. He eats dinner and pretends to be interested. She wants me to fill in the gaps when she can't remember a detail, but I don't remember it either. So, I shrug. I feel like there's nothing I remember much about earlier that afternoon. I can barely remember the entrance I'll have to take tomorrow morning to get to my locker. Which locker was it? Where is the combination?

I try my best to push the questions aside. If I let them linger a little too long, my hands will start shaking again. Instead, I rummage in my memories to find where I saw Kassidy before, but there's no way of accessing those times. They're too far-gone to recall. I make a note to file through old photo albums. Dad gives me sideway glances. I think he's still worried about me. Or maybe he's looking for a sign that I'm different now and I'll start growing tentacles; or maybe that I'll start melting soon from the shock of a lightning bolt.

He says nothing about this morning. And I don't ask.

I go to bed right after dinner. I feel so exhausted, like my entire body was on overdrive all day long. As I lie down and try to fall asleep, flashes of blue light brighten my mind. I give it a second, expecting the flashes to disappear. But they don't.

I open my eyes to make the light go away. I blink helplessly in the darkness of my room, but nothing stops the bright flares in my vision.

I sit up in bed and pull off the covers. I'm cold, and yet I'm dying from heat. I push my legs over the side of my bed, leaning forward. I feel like I'm going to vomit. My stomach is churning.

I wrap myself with my arms, praying that the pain and the lights stop at some point. My legs and arms burn like they're about to rip from my body. I'm sweating from everywhere. I try to scream, but I choke on my voice. Everything hurts. Everything hurts so much.

My eyes roll back, and I let the darkness take me.

*   *   *

In the morning, all the pain is gone. I pretend as though it was all a dream. Everything that's happened to me lately feels like a dream. Nothing feels very real anymore. I walk to the corner of the street where I'm supposed to catch the bus. I'm usually still asleep at this time, so I don't pay much attention to where I'm going. Then I realize there are other people standing near me and one of them is Kassidy.

"Good morning," I say to her, trying my best to sound genuine.

She's probably still sleeping too, because she jumps as though I scared her. "Good morning," she replies in a sigh.

"Sorry I scared you," I apologize.

"Don't worry about it. It's just early," she tells me. "I got used to going to bed late and waking up late. So, this is really early for me."

"I know what you mean," I say, this time it was genuine.

I felt the ground shake for a second. Confused, I look at the others to see if they had any reaction. Perhaps, it's normal here. And I suppose it is because everyone, even Kassidy, ignores it. When I feel the ground shake again, people are more concerned.

"What's going on?" I ask Kassidy, hoping she had the answers.

She seems as confused as I am. She can't answer my question.

The ground shakes again, and again, and again.

A worm crawls into view. It's as big as a house, and as long as a commercial ship. It slinks forward on the street like an accordion, leaving behind a trail of slime. There are rows of razor-sharp teeth at the front, and again at the other extremity. The school bus pulls over just in time: the kids scream and push each other to climb on board.

I'm glued to the spot, distracted by the phenomenon before me. My feet are like boulders melted to the ground beneath me. My hands are shaking wildly and the unsteadiness in my head feels like I'm about to be propelled from my own body.

What the hell is that thing? Is this real, or is it another one of those vivid dreams? I pinch myself to be sure I'm not sleeping.

I'm not sleeping.

It's real. And the reality of it hardly registers in my brain. Because it's impossible.

"Dana, come on," Kassidy calls out from the bus doors.

I try to look away. I take one step back between every tremble caused by the body weight crashing against the asphalt.

The worm travels some way before I'm able to move again. I feel a warm hand touch my elbow.

"Are you okay?" comes Kassidy's soft voice.

"Yeah," I respond. But honestly, I'm not. How can you be alright when the most disgusting creature decides it wants to size-up Ninja Turtle-style and move around town? I'm freaked out! How can a worm get that big? It crawls past us, ignoring us. But where is it going? And where did it come from?

I'm beginning to feel my own heartbeat again when a buzzing noise echoes inside my head. I jump when I hear someone's voice like they were right beside me. I look around me for the source of the voice, but there's only Kassidy. She's looking at me like she's trying to decipher a puzzle.

"Do you hear that?" I ask, while looking around for the source of the many voices that sound both distant and close.

... worm ... too scary ...

... gross ... thing ...

"Hear what?" Kassidy responds. Her face expresses worry, but I can't tell if it's because of the ground shaking, the monster-worm, or if I said something wrong. "I hear the ground shaking, and the kids screaming. What do you hear?"

... freak ... to school ... wanna go home ...

... don't think ... do you ...

"People are talking. They're saying things," I tell her. "I'm hearing them, but I can't make out what they're saying."

Kassidy looks at the kids in the bus, then around us at the houses. I understand from her glare that we're alone, and no one is talking. Perhaps I'm going crazy, but then the voices stop.

"Maybe it was the kids?" I ask Kassidy.

She gently pulls me toward the bus. "I'm pretty sure they're just crying and screaming. But maybe you're right," she says, an eyebrow raised in skepticism.

2

BRYDHEN

The ride to school is uncomfortable. I constantly look outside for any signs of a monster-worm, but there is none. I'm even starting to doubt that it was real at all. But the whining and crying, and whispered conversations in the bus clear my thoughts.

It happened.

And it was real.

So, if it was real, why are we still going to school? I shake the thought away. Why would anyone cancel school, even when there's a monster-worm crawling about the city? They don't even cancel school when there's a winter storm and twenty feet of snow. Why incite panic when we can all pretend it never happened?

When we arrive to school, it's like everyone completely forgets the incident. I question my sanity and my imagination. Was it all just a hallucination? Because moments ago, I thought it was real, but now I feel like it's all in my head. Side effects of being struck by lightning, maybe?

The younger kids stop panicking, because of course the anxiety of Day 1 at school outweighs the sighting of a monster-worm. And as the kids hurry inside the school, someone mentions that their dad works for the city, and they were getting these special effects machines for the upcoming Halloween festival. This seems to make sense to everyone, and of course, seeing their friends and peers for the first time after the summer became the most important thing in the world.

I have to admit, it sort of makes sense. Maybe the city was testing the machine before the festival, which is still two months away. I accept this explanation – it makes much more sense to me than a real monster crawling around. Now I feel silly.

And as I get down from the bus, I feel my own anxiety eating away inside me. The butterflies in my stomach have transformed into millions of eagles trying to rip through my rib cage Alien-style. There's nothing like the unexpectedness of new experiences, seeing everything go wrong in your head before you even walk through the front doors to keep you frozen in place. Despite the fact that I would kill to snuggle under my covers and disappear from the world, I still have to face this. Once the first day is done, it will get easier. I have to believe that.

I don't know anyone except Kassidy, and that makes the emotions rumbling through me even worse. Or better. I can't tell if I'm relieved that at least I know one person, or if it's the most terrible thing on earth. She's not in all my classes so I have to learn to meet people all over again.

I follow Kassidy as we trail behind other students who seem to know where they're going. As we near the entrance, we're welcomed with fumes of smoke. Some guys think they look very cool by leaning on the brown-brick wall, smoking their cigarette, and laughing at stupid things.

I want to cry. I want to die. I want to be anywhere else in the world right now. But I force myself to keep walking, and I cross the threshold. There is no going back now.

And yet, I look back. The bus is already leaving, making way for another school bus to take its place. The bus doors open. A line of students disembarks and heads for the entrance, where I'm standing. I hear the smokers laugh at me because I'm the only idiot standing in the middle of the crowd rushing inside the school. Even though the laughing catches me off guard, I shrug it away. I'm choosing not to care that I'm in the way. Someone has caught my eye. He's taller than me, has dark hair and he's wearing a pair of black jeans, and a black sweater. At first sight, he looks depressed or really estranged, but his military-style haircut and his deep brown eyes tell me otherwise.

I've seen him before. He was standing in front of me yesterday with his dad. As he comes closer, his eyes lock with mine. He marches right in front of me without breaking contact until he's through the doors.

Kassidy comes down the staircase at that precise moment. She sees him and he sees her too. They exchange a glare for a few seconds. Right now, I want to follow him. I want to know who he is, what grade he's in, what classes he has. I want to know all about him. I cross my fingers that he's not younger.

"Dana?" Kassidy calls out. "Are you coming?"

"Yes," I answer, still half-dazed. My anxiety turns suddenly into clear determination. I need to know who that is.

I cross the doors and follow Kassidy to our locker. I look around to get a better idea of what the other students do with their belongings. Mostly, all the others seem to carry their school bags over one shoulder – the cooler look, I suppose. So, I hook my jacket when Kassidy gives me a minute, put away all my binders in the section she decided I would have, and keep only one notebook with me. I decide I don't want to carry my backpack with me, so I hook it over my jacket.

While Kassidy settles her things in the locker, I turn my attention on trying to find the mystery boy with the profound stare. To look less suspicious, I sit down on the bench in front of the locker. Kassidy is still organizing her notebooks, deciding to keep her bag, but then changing her mind. I find it an appropriate time to look around for the young man who captured my gaze. He's not in sight. There are students standing all around the common area running and shouting. I guess they're happy to see each other. There are so many people, and so many unfamiliar faces. As I look on, I get dizzy from the atmosphere and the crowd.

"I know how you feel," Kassidy says. She's sitting beside me now, looking in the same direction as I initially was. "You're looking for someone?"

"No," I answer quickly. "I was just looking."

I hope Kassidy doesn't ask me anything else, especially not about the guy we saw earlier. And then I wonder: if he's not in the senior common area, is he in a different grade? It would be weird that my first crush is younger than me … Maybe crossing my fingers didn't really help.

My heart skips a beat and I swallow nervously at my own thoughts. FIRST CRUSH? I feel really ridiculous. I look down at the purple pen I'm fidgeting with my fingers, failing helplessly to hide my unease. On the outside, I hope I look perfectly normal.

The bell rings. The butterflies in my stomach – or rather those eagles again - are acting up. Kassidy stands with her notebooks and pencil case.

"Where are you going first?" she asks me.

I point at the end of the common area. "French." I'm not excited. I'm nervous to be left alone in a classroom full of unfamiliar people. They would be looking at me and wondering who I am. I genuinely, truly, honestly *hate* being the new girl.

"Good luck," she says to me. She's off to English class.

I nod and walk half-heartedly to the end of the hall, holding onto my notebook like my whole life depended on it. I try to control my breathing, discreetly inhaling and exhaling. I put one foot in front of the other.

I've made it in the classroom. I'm one of the first ones here. Now, my thoughts are in disarray. Should I be here? Am I in the right class? Why isn't anyone else here? What are they waiting for? Should I leave the class, and come back? I choose a seat at the back of the class so that I can inconspicuously check my schedule one more time. I open my notebook cover and slide my finger over my schedule. I find the day and the first period. Yup, I'm in the right place. So why aren't the students coming?

The seconds tick by as a few more students enter the classroom. It's starting to make me feel much better. I try to tell myself that we're in high school; going to your class at the first bell is uncool. Mental note: next time, take your time. I check my schedule again, for good measure. I'm still in the right place.

Finally, the second bell rings and all the other students fill the class. Just as expected, they stare at me like I'm this new, shiny thing to talk about. Compared to other places I've moved to, these teenagers don't care about being subtle. They don't whisper to each other about me. They outright talk about me to each other, while also talking *to* me like I wasn't there. My heart squeezes, but I smile when the students look at me and make comments like, 'hey, she's new,' or 'got a new one, folks.'

The teacher walks in and settles her bag on the desk. She is thin and old. As she piles papers on her desk, I notice the bags under her eyes. She doesn't seem enthusiastic to start a new year. She looks just how I feel: tired and depressed. She doesn't even introduce herself before she starts handing out the class outline.

It's barely been five minutes and I'm bored beyond belief. The teacher literally just reads what she's put on the outline. She begins with the behaviour expectations, obviously. I look around the class and decide that these rules probably don't apply to some of the students sitting around me. I realize I'm the only girl sitting at the back of the class. The other four seats are taken by boys, all of whom are slouching in their seats, their legs spread apart, and their caps turned backward. I guess taking your hat off in the school is not customary here.

The teacher goes through all the important dates, deadlines, and projects. I'm starting to feel nervous again. I'm unprepared – my agenda is still in my locker, and I didn't even bring a highlighter to keep track of the dates. I make a mental note to put all the deadlines in my agenda later at home. I think I'm better off doing it at home anyway, so I don't look like a total nerd on my first day at a new school. The thought alone decreases my blood pressure.

I start to doodle on the corner of the class outline. A little flower here and there. A vine edging its way up the page, with small or large-sized leaves, unevenly spread out on the vine. I wane in and out of attention, just enough to realize when we're turning the page.

By the time the bell for recess rings, I feel like I've calmed down, like I can breathe a little easier. But I'm so exhausted. The class was dreadfully long and pointless. It took an entire hour just to go through the outline, and we did nothing at all. Maybe that's why classes here take up the entire year, and not just a semester.

According to my schedule, I have a fifteen-minute break. I leave the classroom and head back to the bench in front of my locker. Within a minute, Kassidy is sitting beside me. "How was your first class?" she asks me candidly. "I totally forgot my agenda earlier, so I think I'll get organized later at home."

I look at her, raising my eyebrows.

"What?" she says, giggling. "Don't judge. I've got control issues."

I chortle genuinely. "No, no," I retort, loosening my grip on my notebook and my pen. "I was literally thinking the exact same thing earlier in class." I suddenly feel super at ease. We have a lot more in common than I thought.

Kassidy raises an eyebrow like she does when she's sceptical, but this time, she has a slight smile and gives me a sideways glance. She reminds me of an anime character, but I won't tell her that. What if she judges me for watching anime like it's no longer a cool thing to do?

"Got a question," I say instead.

"Shoot," she tells me, while opening her binder rings and placing the outline of her previous class under the first tab. She's getting super organized. Control issues, she says? I like her already; I think we're going to be good friends.

"Are there always two bells before a class?" I inquire, lowering my voice so that I'm not overheard and made fun of by someone else.

"Euh," Kassidy starts. "Yeah, I think so. I think most people really hear the second bell."

"What do you mean?" I reply, trying to see if she's come to the same conclusion as me.

"First bell is for the nerds who want to go to class, and the second bell is for … well, everyone else," she tells me, a sly look in her eyes.

I smile. "Right."

I expect math to be the same way as French class. But it's not. I'm shocked and uncomfortable. First, the teacher seems to take herself rather seriously. She's kind of short, a little like me, but she stands her ground. I assume she's had to over the years of teaching, since most of her male students stand a few heads over her. I'd be intimidated too. Even though all the students have chosen their seats, she makes us stand up and then assigns the seats in alphabetical order.

The more she calls the students' names, the more I pray I won't be sitting in the front. And then I see him. The boy who caught my eye earlier this morning – he's standing at the front of the class, among some of the other, much taller boys of the class. By the way he is getting glances from some of the girls, I'm assuming he is new to this school too. When he catches my eye again, I look away.

My heart almost jumped into my throat for a second there.

The teacher finally calls my name. My seat is the one right beside the classroom door, second to last in the row. And to my terror, I'm sitting right in front of the striking stranger. He tries to catch my eye, but I don't dare look at him. I settle in my seat wishing to god he isn't staring at the back of my head, or worse, the bottom of my back where my shirt lifts a tiny bit to reveal some skin. I just can't help it, and I pull on the back of my shirt, in case.

The teacher's seating plan feels like it takes forever as she finally reaches the bottom of the student list. She gives us all the course outline and starts robotically reading through it. I swallow my gut as I try to follow along, but it sounds like she's reading gibberish. I understand literally nothing of what she's talking about – something about trigonometry and precalculus complex equations. To me, it sounds like the teacher's words and the words written in front of me are one puzzle on top of another. I feel my heartbeat accelerate and my palms getting both sweaty and cold at the same time. I try to keep face and pretend like I'm following along, but the seasickness in my head overwhelms all my other senses.

The guy sitting on my left constantly glares my way. I know he's not criticizing me. He's simply figuring out who I am. He's just a little bit taller than me. I can tell just by the way he's sitting: on the edge of his chair, his back straight to look taller. He's wearing a pair of blue jeans a little too big for him, and a plain orange T-shirt. His features aren't necessarily attractive, due to his acne. But he's cute in his own way. I realize I've seen him before. His clothes-matching skills aren't better from one day to the other. I wonder if he ever found the person he wanted to give the very expensive gift to.

The class goes by far too slowly for my taste. And when the bell rings, I scramble out quickly and make my way back to the bench in front of my locker. I finally feel like I release my grip on my notebook. A part of me wants to rip apart the math course outline while the other part of me obsesses on how I'll somehow get a grip on myself and figure it out. Still, an illogical fear sucks the life right out of my veins.

"Are you okay?" Kassidy asks me when she sits beside me. I was so focused on my own terror that I didn't see her return from her class.

"I think so," I answer, letting the sensation of relief flood through me.

Kassidy's presence alone makes me feel a lot better already.

Kassidy raises an eyebrow. "Math?"

I nod sheepishly. "Yeah," I admit. "I think I just saw hell for the first time."

Kassidy grins at my response, but I know she would have laughed if she didn't already empathize with the torture I just experienced. "We can go to the administration together later, get you transferred to my class instead."

I look over at her. I'm surprised and a little flabbergasted. She's kinda really cool.

We sit together in silence, and I watch Kassidy colour-code her math assignments and units for the school year. When the bell rings at the end of the 15-minute break, Kassidy and I walk together to biology class. She lets me choose where we'll be sitting, and I choose the row at the back of the class.

The class is made up of laboratory long tables, and on each edge of the class, there are lab stations equipped with microscopes, beakers, test tubes in racks, and dissecting sets. I decide to sit at the end of the long table, closest to the middle row. As the other students file in, I don't recognize anyone from my previous two classes. I'm confused, but I know I'm in the right place because Kassidy is with me.

I turn to her right away. "I don't see anyone from our grade," I tell her.

"Yeah, I know," Kassidy agrees. "We've been placed in the bio class for the year below us. I think they did that because we moved here from another province."

"Ah," I say, accepting her explanation. If I had a choice, I'd counter that decision, but I'm beginning to feel a throbbing sensation at my temples, so I let it go for now. I change the subject immediately. "The guy we saw earlier," I tell her. "He's new too, right?"

"I think so," Kassidy responds, already knowing who I'm talking about. "Why?"

"He's in my math class," I share. Kassidy raises her eyebrows, but it's like there's a sparkle in her eyes that worries me for a second.

Before Kassidy has the chance to answer me, the teacher walks through the door. She's well rounded and small. She wears a red and white striped long-sleeve shirt. It's very distracting and hard to look at for very long. The teacher speaks and the class falls silent.

Kassidy rips a piece of paper from her notebook and scribbles something on it. She slides the paper over to me.

Should we go talk to the guy tomorrow?

I search for my pen and respond: *Why?*

While Kassidy writes something, I look up to see the teacher, but her shirt is making my headache much worse. So, I return my attention to the piece of paper that's being passed to me.

Because it would be nice to have another friend? Maybe he's alone.

I look over at Kassidy. She's smiling as though she came up with the brightest idea. I can't help but smile back. She's funny. So, I nod in response to her message and whisper, "tomorrow."

Kassidy takes back the paper and begins to doodle. She draws mostly stars and stickmen. I take a paper of my own. I can't think of anything to draw except for anime girls. Over the years, I practiced that type of cartoon, and it became a second nature. I feel Kassidy's stare on me as my hand and pencil slide over the paper to create an anime character. When I'm done, only ten minutes of the class elapsed.

"Another one," Kassidy says under her breath.

I smile at my paper and draw another anime girl. By the end of the class, I drew a whole sorority, and Kassidy decides she's going to keep it all. We barely listened to the teacher. But we didn't need to. The material she was presenting was known knowledge for both Kassidy and me. We learned it where we used to live before. Due to this system, Kass and I have to take biology again. It's going to be a long year in biology.

The bell rings. All the students storm out of the classroom and head to their lockers. Kassidy and I put our books away. And that's when I see the stranger again. His locker is approximately in the middle of the section. He looks so serious. And he talks to no one. Perhaps Kassidy is right: maybe he's alone.

Kassidy realizes where I'm looking. She closes the locker door and elbows me. "Go," she says.

"I thought we agreed tomorrow," I retort. I'm really nervous.

"Just go!" she replies with a small push at my back.

"Why do I have to talk to him?" My mouth is dry, and my palms are sweaty. The sound around me is starting to feel far away.

"Because I had the idea," Kassidy says, proud of herself.

She pushes me along a few more feet. Before I know it, I'm standing right behind him. I try to swallow, but there is nothing in my mouth. I hold my breath hoping maybe it will freeze the butterflies in my stomach or stop my heart from beating so fast.

I lift my finger and poke his shoulder. The stranger turns around. Once again, his eyes lock with mine. I'm paralyzed, lost in the dark colour of his eyes.

"Hi," I say quickly, finding my voice.

"Hi back," he says. His voice is deep and manly. I never heard a voice like his.

"I'm Dana. This is Kassidy. We're new here."

"Me too."

"What's your name?"

"Brydhen."

"We have to go. But we'll see you tomorrow?"

"Sure."

And that was the fastest introduction ever. As I walk away, I start to feel my heart fuel the throbbing in my temple, and I taste a bit of sour in my mouth. I pack my bag in silence. I know that Kassidy is saying something – a lot of somethings – but I can't hear her. I'm too focused on the shaking of my hands and trying to calm myself down. By the time I follow Kassidy to our bus, my hands are dry, my mouth is hydrated, and I feel like less of a zombie.

"He's cute," Kassidy says as we sit down. "But he doesn't chat much."

"No. I felt really awkward," I confess.

"It won't be as weird tomorrow," she reassures.

"Let's hope …"

KASSIDY

3
KASSIDY'S REVELATION

I lie in bed wondering what in the world is happening to me. Is it exciting or is it mind-blowing? Maybe it's a bit of both. If I think about it, it all started on the night I got struck by lightning. I can't even imagine if I'm just really lucky or really unlucky. I seriously thought for a while that some higher power wanted to make me pay for something, like somehow, I deserved a punishment straight from the sky. But turns out I wasn't the only one. I know this for a fact because I overheard some of the doctors talking the night I was hospitalized – there was someone else who was struck by lightning at the same time as me. So … is it really coincidence? It sure doesn't seem like it. I mean, I'm not the kind of person who believes in karma or fate, but honestly, how is it possible that two people get struck by lightning at the exact same time? It's not possible. It just can't be.

    I swear I've never been so scared in my life than the night I was released from the hospital. It was like a dream, but I obviously wasn't dreaming. I flew! Like in the air, wind-under-my-arms-and-defying-gravity kind of flying! I tried to control my body as it lifted into the air, Newton's Law slowly releasing its grip on me. But I had to let go – it just felt … natural. Almost instinctual.

I flew around the sky all night. I discovered I could control my speed, the height of my flight, and the direction I wanted to take. Yeah, okay, I freaked out first. But then it became too real to ignore. I spun around, whirled like nobody's business, going faster and slower. I can't even describe the feeling of freedom, happiness and tranquility. Nothing's ever been so peaceful in my life like the wind rustling through my hair and the feeling of cold air on my skin.

A while after my excitement faded, I felt like someone was watching me. But that was impossible. Right? Like, I was hundreds of meters above the tallest building. But the whole idea that I was flying in the first place, that was even more impossible. I was very much aware of what was happening. I know it was real.

Tonight, I plan to fly for the third time. I love the feeling it gives me: freedom, and space between my sister, Dad, and me. We keep fighting over meaningless things, like the way I walked into the house and the tone I took with Mom, or the way my sister bothers me with her loud music when I'm trying to watch TV. It feels so good to have my own space that no one in the world can reach.

Earlier, I snuck out of my room. I didn't want my parents to know I was leaving. I wouldn't know what to tell them, and they would probably forbid me to leave since it was a school night, and it was passed ten. But I made it to the backyard.

I'm standing in the dark, scared of getting caught by my parents. I'm trying not to make a sound. I gather my courage and strength, and I shoot into the air with no hesitation, leaving everything behind. I go higher and higher. I close my eyes and let the air try to slow me down or push against me. Nothing can stop me. I slow down to a halt just under the rain clouds. I'm showered with tiny drops of water as I take in the city's lights below me.

Nothing, not the wind or the cold, bothers me. Nothing in the world can take this newfound freedom from me. I breathe in the night air feeling invincible. I venture the sky, go as far as I like, and travel for as long as I want to. I practice movements and turns. I slow down, go faster, and stop. I let my body drop with the gravity. As my body rushes toward the ground, I regain control and shoot back into the air again.

A few hours pass, and I decide to return home. I speed toward the ground feet first. I slow down almost to a stop, and slowly descend to the ground for a soft landing. Proud of myself, I quietly walk to my room and go to bed. I feel badass.

Before I close the blinds of my window, I look at the sky one more time. Sunrise is in an hour. I promise next time I'll stay out to see it from high above the rest of the world.

I wake up very tired a few hours later. My day starts off bad: I wake up late with a headache, and I can't find my hairbrush. After a few minutes of searching, I catch a glimpse of the handle under a pile of papers on my computer desk. It *has* to be on the other side of my room to make me move as much as possible. I see a person to my left as I walk by the mirror. I jump at the reflection. It doesn't belong to me.

Who is that person?

I look down at myself, then back at the stranger in the mirror. My heart clenches. We look exactly alike. The person I see is wearing black booty shorts under a long orange-rust skirt, opened from the right upper thigh down to the floor, bordered with a white stripe. She wears simple white boots. She's wearing a nice, yet simple, orange-rust tank-top.

The girl in the mirror breathes at the same time I do. I take a step back, and she does too. I'm wearing her clothes. I *am* her! White fingerless gloves, white-laced black armbands on my upper arms, and a silver mask to hide my eyes. My hair is now bright ginger, just as long as before, but with bangs. I look so much different than my real self. I'm so confused.

I panic.

"Shit! Shit! Shit! Shit! Shit! What is happening? Can't I have a normal identity crisis? Shit! Shit! Shit! This really sucks! I HAVE TO CATCH THE BUS!"

After a few short breaths, I'm resolved to calm down. But I'm so confused. I don't know what's going on. "Okay … calm down, Kass," I tell myself. I sit down on my bed and close my eyes. I try to relax as much as possible, and to control my breathing. I open my eyes again, and reluctantly look in the mirror. There I am again: my normal self.

I'm shocked. I don't know what to think anymore. I don't know if I should be scared, nervous, or delighted. My head is pounding. I don't feel like doing anything today. Not even go to school. I just want to know what's happening to me. I want someone to tell me everything is going to be okay, and that it's not my fault. I want someone to tell me I didn't cause these changes, and I will soon find out why it's all happening to me. I want someone to reassure me that they made a mistake somewhere, and these powers are supposed to belong to someone else.

"Kassidy! Your bus is passing soon! Hurry up!" Mom shouts from the hall.

Her voice brings me back to reality. The reality I don't like: the one where I have to go to school and keep everything a secret. I hurry to get ready. A thought crosses my mind while I'm running around my room for my jacket. It would be convenient to teleport where I want when I'm late, like the bus stop for example.

I turn around quickly to reach for my doorknob, but it's no longer there. Instead, there are people standing at the corner of the street. The wind has time to blow in my hair and disappear before I understand that I'm outside … and at the bus stop with the other students.

"Are you okay? You look pale," Dana asks. She's standing not too far from me. She approaches me, concerned.

"What? Oh … yes, yes! I'm okay," I mumble. I look back, half expecting to see my bedroom. Instead, I see my mom looking at me from the doorframe a few houses away.

"Are you sure?"

"Yes. I'm all right. I just have a little bit of a headache," I reply with a quick smile. It's better if I'm at school anyways. It's a break from the tense atmosphere at home.

"I have headaches every day," Dana says. "Ever since …"

"Ever since what?" I ask.

"Nothing. Never mind," she replies.

She's keeping something from me. And as curious as I am to find out what it is, I'm not going to pressure. We don't know each other well enough for that. And I have secrets of my own. Another person lives inside me! And it appeared to me this morning. Why?

What's happening to me?

Constant headaches. Flying. Teleportation on demand.

I want to scream right now. I'm panicking. But I can't let the rest of the world see what I'm becoming. I have no one to talk to about this. Who am I supposed to approach? Am I supposed to keep it all bottled up inside? Let all these feelings rot inside me and explode when I won't be able to hold it in anymore? What am I supposed to do? Am I supposed to understand that these changes are normal or natural? They're not at all! It's *super*natural if anything!

I follow Dana in the bus. I keep my thoughts to myself during the ride to school and ignore Dana's worried glares. I escape my reverie and zombie-state once at school where all the chatter and the noise flood my ears. I wasn't even aware that we arrived at school already.

"Will you be alright?" Dana asks me. "You look really pale ... like you've seen a ghost."

"Yeah, I'm okay," I tell her. "What's your first class?"

"English. You?"

"History," I answer.

We sit down together on the bench opposite our locker and avoid looking at each other. I don't know why, though. I guess because I'm keeping something from her, and she knows it.

"Did you find out anything about the giant worm we saw yesterday?" Dana questions.

"Yeah. It was all over the internet," I respond. "Videos and such. But no one knows what it was."

"It's strange that no one knows anything about it," says Dana.

I agree. It was really strange.

"Where did it come from, you think?" I ask her.

"Not from around here, that's for sure," Dana replies. "Still finding it hard to believe it was a Halloween prop. It's not really family-friendly-looking."

"Agreed," I say to her.

The bell rings and I'm glad to be away from prying eyes. I feel like everyone is looking at me, like I've become the center of attention – maybe because they know what I'm hiding. No, don't be silly, Kass. It's probably the dumb look on my face as I fight back the throbbing in my frontal lobe.

As I part ways with Dana, I catch a glimpse of Brydhen. He seems spaced out. I follow his stare and realize he's looking at Dana. I wish someone would look at me that way too. There's definitely something between them. And he's really cute. I have to admit Dana is lucky. He would never look at me that way, even if I wanted him too. And I want him too. But he doesn't see me at all. All his energy and attention are focused on her. Not on me.

Why not *me*?

Is it because their eyes met first? Is it because she's prettier than me? I rather just think he's superficial, and he likes the outside better than the inside. If he's that way, then I won't bother with him.

I hate history class. That's why I prefer to sit at the back, so the teacher won't see me doodle on paper, or ignore him completely throughout his lecture. I prepare pen and paper, just in case I need it.

"Hi everyone. I'm Robert Gray and I'll be your history teacher this year," says a fifty-year-old man with salt and pepper hair, blue navy shirt and black pants.

He's explaining where he comes from, what he plans on doing this semester, and his goals as a teacher. It all sounds very good, but it interests no one. Every student in the class is already focused on something else:

themselves, probably – because I'm focused on myself too. I feel bad for the teacher. It hasn't even been five minutes.

My head is pounding. I hear the ticking of the minutes from the clock behind me. It sounds a hundred times louder than it really is. My vision blurs as my head thumps harder. I take off my glasses and rub my eyes. I look around the class and find details I didn't see before.

The black board has never been greener.

The dents in the tables have never been sharper.

I have never *seen* clearer!

As amazed as I am, the headache only worsens. I reach into my bag to find anything that can help me. The shuffling bothers the teacher, and I find nothing useful.

I lift my hand in desperation.

"Yes?" Mr. Gray asks me.

"May I be excused? I don't feel very well," I explain, wincing from the pain.

"Sure," he answers, unaware of the protocol in this situation.

As I stand, the room spins and accelerates with each step I take. The students' voices disappear. Everything goes black.

4

TRANSFORMATION

I wake up in the school infirmary. When the tall but plump nurse notices I'm awake, she approaches my bed. Her large, stubby fingers grab my forearm, then she places two fingers on my wrist and checks her watch. The nurse raises her dark, thick eyebrows, but I can't tell if she's satisfied by the result, or suspicious. She reaches over on the counter next to her and forces a glass of water in my hand. I take the hint and sit up to drink.

"How are you feeling, Miss Avalon?" she asks me.

"Better, I guess," I answer. Honestly, I don't know what to respond. Should I tell her I think I'm turning into a mutant with superpowers?

"Have you been sleeping well?" the nurse questions, staring into my eyes.

Is she trying to catch a lie?

"Not really," I tell her. "Nightmares and such." The truth is still too far-fetched to discuss: I spend my nights sneaking out of my house and flying free in the sky until early morning.

"I see," she says, and walks over to her desk. She picks up the phone and dials three numbers. "Hello Nadine, will you contact Ms. Avalon's parents? She's going home for the rest of the day." She hangs up.

"Why are you sending me home?" I ask her. I don't want to go home. That will leave Dana and Brydhen alone, and I won't see what will happen. The headache is gone. I can stay now.

"Your eyes are weird, and you need to get a few more hours of sleep today and tonight. That's why I'm sending you home," she retorted with an attitude. She gives me the impression she really doesn't like working with teenagers.

"What's wrong with my eyes?" I question, looking around the room for a mirror. But there doesn't seem to be one.

"Nothing to be concerned about," she replies to close the conversation.

But it's enough to send me home. I try to understand her mixed signals, but I don't get her logic. I'd rather stay at school. I'll miss a lot if I don't stay. I won't be able to watch Dana and Brydhen.

"Get your eyes checked, though? I think your headache is due to the fact that you don't need your glasses," the nurse tells me.

Where did she get her diploma? If I have glasses, that means I need them. I touch my face by habit to push up my glasses. They're not there. Where are they? I look around the room and see them resting on the bedside table. I reach for them but freeze halfway.

I'm not wearing my glasses.

I can see clearly.

I smile. I had to wear glasses since the age of twelve. Now that's over.

I'm starting to like all these changes happening to me. Mostly, they have me freaked out and scared. But once I get used to them, like the flying part, I like it. Very much. I can barely keep up with how quickly the changes are happening. That's probably why some changes cause me a lot of pain, like headaches and such.

And after all that, the only question that seems to bother me is the identity of the person I saw in my mirror this morning. Of all things to be worried about, that's the one that nags at me. Not the fact that I can now fly, that my eyes have somehow healed, or that teleportation is possible. No. None of that.

I'm worried about what I think to be my alter ego. If I think about it long enough, I don't feel convinced that the transformation happened at all. But if I believe everything else that's happening, why can't I believe this too?

Was it because I was struck by lightning? And if so, can these things happen to other people struck by lightning too? No. People don't get superpowers from lightning. Right? So, why did I? Why *me*?

*   *   *

Rest, my ass, Nurse Janet. I soar higher and higher until the clouds are below me. I watch as an airplane crosses the sky and disappears in the distance. The world can't touch me up here. I breathe in the smell of freedom and peace.

Those feelings don't last very long. The image of the person in my mirror invades my thoughts. Is it really me? If it is, then I should be able to access that person. The thought alone of calling forth that individual gives me butterflies. But I guess I must. I need to know if she's real. I need to see who she is. It makes me nervous as hell, and I'm really freaked to see what's going to happen. But I won't sleep at night until I do.

I close my eyes and try to concentrate. But I don't know what to concentrate on. I feel something burning in my chest. I clutch my shirt and find the burning sensation getting stronger. In my mind's eye, I see her. I see me. I open my eyes. To my great disappointment (and some comfort), I'm still me. But the pain doesn't stop.

The cloud below me forms a twister. Faster and faster, it spins. The wind and the pressure of the twister pull me inside. I'm drenched with water. I feel like my chest is bursting open. My entire body feels on fire. Gold rings encircle my head and feet. It looks like it's the clouds doing it, but I know it's not. It only takes a second, and the ring above me makes its way to my feet, and the one at my feet moves to my head. And there she is. There I am. The person I saw in the mirror this morning. She's here!

I'm no longer Kassidy. I'm now the other me, the one who has been residing in me. I look like someone else, and yet, feel like me.

I hover in the cloud, wet and cold. I take a look around me. My mask feels like a part of my skin. It does not affect my vision in the least. I drop a few feet out of the cloud. It's time to face reality. I'm simply in disguise.

Superheroes exist.

And I am one.

5

SURROUNDED

A rush of energy shivers through me. It makes me anxious and alarmed. My stomach churns and my palms are sweaty.

Yet again, another thing is happening to me that I don't understand.

A shadow flies under me. I see it through the cloud below. Whatever it is, I can tell it's fast. Faster than a bird for sure. I obey my gut feeling and drop a few more feet through the clouds below me. I watch the shadow in the distance soar with great speed. I fly in pursuit as quickly as possible. I catch up within seconds, thanks to all those hours of flying practice. It's not too far ahead. I can see the shadow quite well now.

I pump the breaks in mid-air, too shocked as I realize what I'm looking at – or rather – *who* I'm looking at. It's a person!

The stranger stops abruptly and turns around to face me. Although we have a few yards between us I can tell that she's staring me down. We stare at each other. She has long, black hair and a silver mask just like mine. She wears black jeans with red flames on each side and at the bottom. Her top is very dusky pink. It looks like a sport's bra with transparent material underneath, opened at the center.

The girl breaks our glare when she suddenly drops to the ground. She looks really skilled at that. No fear either. As she drops from the air, her body is completely straight, but her arms are above her head. I can't help but smile slightly. I thought about doing that myself, but I thought I'd look too silly. But it's clearly easier to drop in height without forcing your arms to stay at your side.

I speed toward her, but not as fast. We land, still facing each other. We're downtown on a street not very occupied on this late afternoon. It's located beside a fence and train tracks. I'm waiting for her to say something, but she keeps quiet and very still. I have the feeling she knows something I don't.

The ground shakes. But not like the time I saw the worm. It's quite different. This time, it feels like a rumbling beneath. It feels like the earth is angry. The street fractures between us. We hold our balance while a chasm slices the street in half. The crevasse slowly snakes toward me and between my feet. I look over my shoulder as the crack continues further on.

All goes quiet.

I look to the girl for answers. But she looks just as serious as ever. An explosion from behind shocks me. I lean forward, covering my head. Large blocks of cement fly in all directions. A piece falls to my left, too close for comfort. I look up and see the girl stand as though she's prepared for something to attack her. She looks ready for a fight.

I slowly turn around.

A dark form towers over me. It hides the sunset and the light. It looks at me with terrible white eyes. I hold my breath, trembling from fright. I'm sure this is my last moment on earth. I'm certain something horrible is about to happen to me. Arms detach from the shape. Great threatening arms and fingers grow.

The sun's last sunrays hit my face without warning. I blink awkwardly, and my eyes adjust easily. I take a look around me. The creature is now splattered against the railway fence. It is made of brown guck, or slime, with a head, eyes, arms, and fingers. But it has no legs. It crawls to travel. And it's now immobile against the fence. The slime is gradually falling off.

The girl is standing right beside the scene. I realize she came to my rescue. She must have pushed the creature away.

"Thank you," I tell her.

She doesn't answer. She doesn't even look at me. She seems mesmerized by the creature.

We watch silently as the guck falls to the ground. The strangest scream I've ever heard in my life. The girl and I look around for the source of the noise. From the corner appears the biggest and hairiest spider ever. Like, ever. It's the size of a blue whale, if that whale also has enormous, hairy legs.

At least, it's not a worm, I think to myself.

Its legs are quick and quiet. The teeth snap at the front as the arachnid sees us.

"Oh shit," is all I can muster. I'm out of words. I don't know what I'm supposed to do.

"Fuck," the girl says. It's the first word I hear from her, and it doesn't sound good. I look at what bothers her. The pile of brown slime is gone. Instead, it took the form it previously had.

I'm scared shitless. The girl and me … we're surrounded with creatures that should not exist.

"What do we do now?" I ask her, ready for anything.

"I'll take the giant," she tells me. In a split second she's gone. She's gliding over the ground in a hurry to attain her opponent.

I turn around and gulp. My heart is beating so fast in my chest I swear it's about to rip out. I wipe my sweaty hands on my skirt. I have to accept my situation and turn my intuition into fighting skills.

I take a stance and prepare for battle.

6
FIRST FIGHT

The slime monster launches an arm forward in an attempt to wrap its fingers around my throat. Luckily, my body is faster than my thoughts. I jump up. My body wheels in the air and I land. Surprised, I find myself facing the fence. I whirl around quickly.

Somehow, I avoided being strangled, let alone touched by that *thing*. And as I pay closer attention to my own feelings, a realization comes to me. I'm trembling and my fists are clenched, but my fear is gone.

I watch in horror as the back of the slime monster squirms and becomes the front, forcing me to stare into those white eyes. They send goosebumps down my spine.

The sun is now out of sight, plunging us in early evening light. The sky is dimming slowly. I'm scared I won't be able to see my opponent once night falls. From where I stand, the other fighter doesn't seem to care. She's doing pretty well for herself. She's hovering in the air, punching the spider's many eyes, rendering it blind and vulnerable to other attacks. The giant squeals of pain and is stepping madly from side to side. It's trying desperately to get away from the girl and trying to bite her at the same time.

The shrieking distracts the slime monster. I wonder if I should run away now while I have the chance, or attack while the creature is sidetracked. My head is telling me I should escape, but my body and the shivers on my arms want me to stay and fight. The feeling is almost unbearable. It's like the super girl in me knows what she must do, and she *really* wants to do it.

A spotlight from the news helicopter above shoots down on us. I am blinded for only a second. My vision adjusts quickly to the flashes of blue light, and then return to darkness. The fear that I won't see my opponent fades as I learn to trust my eyes. They won't let me down.

The slime monster isn't paying attention to me anymore. There are other things much more interesting around. It hurls an arm up quicker than I can see, then stands with its arms now limp on his sides. And it looks at me. I swear it seems like he's smiling. But I can't be sure until …

An explosion overhead scares me. I look up and find the helicopter blown to bits. A large fire, that I guess is the body of the flying vehicle, plummets to the ground. Members of the helicopter plunge in our direction. I stare in disbelief. People were in there. They couldn't have survived. I feel a pang of anger and sadness within me. I can't believe it blew up innocent people!

My attention darts back to the monster. I feel the need to blow it to smithereens too. My head goes through a series of torture exercises when suddenly, sparks of pain shoot through my body. I look at the source of the pain and find my arm gashed. The cut seems really deep. My anger must have distracted me from the fiery bits of helicopter falling from the sky. The wound starts to swell immediately. My skin burns and turns black and blue from the impact of the hot metal. I grab my arm from the pain.

All I need is a bit more time to recollect myself and pull my thoughts together to figure out what I'm going to do. The blood oozes down my arm and between my fingers, forming a puddle at my feet. I barely have time to think, because my head is spinning from the loss of blood, before the slime monster launches another attack. This time, it's toward me.

I duck as his fist flies over my head. The next second, my face is flat against the cement ground. I pull myself up on my knees, feeling the burning sensation in my arm. It's beginning to numb from the pain. The buildings around are dancing left and right in the moonlight. I touch my nose. It's bleeding. And it's really crooked.

I'm frightened at the idea of what will come next. Will I be beat to death? Am I going to die right here? Will my new and sharp instincts be able to save me? Will I lose consciousness from the dizziness? My heart pulses rapidly in my chest at the very idea of my end. I never thought about death before, and the sudden realization that it may be looming around the corner has me in a state of internal panic, because on the outside, I must look stunned and ridiculous. I'm staring at my bloody fingers.

I get up and remind myself that attacks from the front can bounce back. The fight has barely begun that I already feel knocked out of the ring. But I try to stand my ground anyway. In normal circumstances, I would drop down, cry, and plead that all this just goes away. But I've finally accepted that this is my fate. I have to be strong and act like a hero – although right now, I'm not much of one. If someone's life lay in the balance, they would probably be dead because of me. Because I'm not doing anything. I haven't even tried to attack yet. So, what am I waiting for? Am I too much of a coward to confront this creature?

Shaking my thoughts away, I decide I have to go for it. If my life were at stake, I would want my hero to save me and not just stand there looking silly. I'm going to at least try to defend myself.

The slime monster awkwardly slides over to me. Things around me stop dancing, and my vision is back to normal in the nick of time. The creature is only a few feet from me. My heart threatens to send fear through me again. But

I'm not willing to let it control me. Although my arm feels like it may fall off at any moment, I steady myself and –

I stab my fist into the slime. I suppose what I aimed at was its chest, but I can't be sure what with all the wiggling and moving of the slime. The guck cascades around my fist, and the monster laughs as though nothing happened. At least, I think it's a laugh. It sounded more like a gurgling. I pull out my hand before I lose it somewhere in the body of mud.

"Predzellmoo not urt," it boomed. Or that's what I heard.

I dare to ask: "What did you say?" I actually didn't want it to escape my mouth, but it was too hard to hold in.

"PREDZELLMOO NOT URT," it pronounced again, this time louder. It didn't want me to miss what it was saying.

"Your name is Predzellmoo?" I question, careful with my tone. I don't want to make it angry. But my arm is throbbing with ache, so my tone might have disclosed my irritation and discomfort in the whole situation.

I still can't make out the rest of its sentence, nor its intentions. Is it trying to be friendly? Is it making fun of me?

"NOT URT," it roars again.

This time, my head is able to translate. This time, I get it. It's not hurt. I didn't hurt it with my punch.

"We'll see about that," I retort back.

I quickly scan around me for any type of weapon, anything I can use for self-defense. The closest thing I find is the thing that hurt my arm: a sort of joystick that looks like a control device. I pick it up and throw it at my opponent.

"Catch that," I cry. I stay locked in position as the creature does exactly that: it catches it. Sort of …

Because I threw it from such short distance, the slime monster, Predzellmoo, didn't have time to lift its hand properly. The stick penetrated its palm. At this point, I have a bad feeling. I take a few steps back. The creature meanwhile simply stares at the stick for a moment. It seems confused or dazed. But it doesn't move. I slowly put more space between us. It pulls out the stick. This tells me the creature is literally made of slime. There's no body underneath it all!

I force my last meal back down, but I can't stop the uncontrollable gag. I'm disgusted as the mud falls off the stick in chunks, like really wet poop.

"DIS YORS," it belches loudly.

It throws the stick back at me, but with no force at all. I put my uninjured arm up to protect my face and wonder why the creature isn't *trying* to hurt me.

I must look very confused right now because the slime monster cocks its head to the side. It's staring me down with those big, white eyes. I continue to back away, but then find there's no more space behind me. I'm right up against the fence. And then it smiles. Shivers crawl down my spine and I feel something is terribly wrong with this picture.

DANA

7

AWARENESS

I catch my breath while the spider-monster looks for me around the corner of the glass building. The sensation flowing through me right now makes me think of this morning. I had a feeling something strange was going to happen. I can't really explain it. That feeling in the pit of my stomach this morning was unmistakable – there was something in the air, and it felt wrong. I was so focused on that feeling that I must have looked like I was staring into outer space – standing there alone at the bus stop.

One second, I was wondering if Kassidy was going to make it in time to the bus stop, all the while staring at her house. The next second, I was hit with this crazy feeling like something was wrong.

For that precise moment, I was so sure there was someone nearby – an enormously powerful someone – someone I should know. And then Kassidy was in front of me at the bus stop like she'd been there the whole time.

She didn't look too good. I didn't want to pry because we weren't that close yet, but I couldn't help it. She looked like she'd seen a ghost. Kass told me she had a headache, and I almost revealed that I often had headaches too, ever since I was hit by lightning. But my internal alarm held me back. That was something I didn't want to share this early in our friendship. She would probably think I was a freak, seeing as I survived a major shock. The thought alone of sharing something so personal brought on a series of squeezes in my gut, anxiety filling any happy space in my soul. Kassidy would probably stop talking to me altogether. That wouldn't be new to me, anyway.

Later that day, I found out Kassidy went home because she fainted in history class. I knew she looked a little pale …

I was sitting in silence with Brydhen for lunch. Every few seconds, I wanted to lose myself in those beautiful, brown eyes staring back at me. But then there was the awkwardness of high school noises around us, the banter of some guy pretending he doesn't want the experience of a deep, romantic love, and the squealing laughter of yet another girl flirting at a terrible joke. Despite all that, Brydhen's stare was steady. It made my heart beat harder and faster, and my palms sweat. I couldn't eat my lunch. My head was spinning. I felt high – a liberating and light feeling I wasn't used to.

So maybe being with Brydhen was a good thing. He made me feel at ease and normal. Everything else about high school or the torment in my stomach vanished.

Unfortunately, I had to leave lunch early. At first, I thought his presence was making me lightheaded. I stumbled to the girl's bathroom and to my luck, found it empty. I locked myself in the last cubicle and leaned against the wall.

That's where my suffering began.

That's where my questions were answered.

My body was trembling from the cold shivers and the heat rising in my chest. I regurgitated my sandwich and apple pie. I felt like my skin was on fire. I struggled to keep my screams locked in my throat. My breathing was out of control. I was damp with sweat. I stood up, clinging to my shirt and regaining balance on the wall.

I lifted my hands to wipe the sweat from my cheeks. I found a mask covering my eyes. It was glued to my face and so thin I could barely difference it from my skin. My hair was much longer and darker now. But the surprise of this transformation was not enough to distract me from the pain writhing through me, to the ends of my fingers, to my toes.

A gold light blinded me, forcing my eyes closed. I wanted to pass out or die and let my body be consumed by this fire. But it didn't. Instead, a rush of energy pulled me into the air, through the ceiling and into the clouds.

Within moments, I discovered my true self, the one that was in me the whole time. The unique uniform, the flying abilities, and the power were all involved to make me what I am now. But how long had it been hiding away? Was I supposed to become like this at this particular moment in my life?

My thoughts on my super-identity were cut short when it occurred to me that I could still be in bed, dreaming of impossible things. That was a more probable scenario, because in reality, superheroes don't exist. And this was real life. That made more sense. The only thing I've come to accept is that I could fly. Now and then, even that was hard to believe. It felt so unreal when I thought back on my expeditions in the sky. Was some of it real? Was this truly happening to me? A part of me wanted to believe it was, that I was special in some way, and important to the world. The other part of me was laughing at my childishness.

Grow up, Dana. This isn't you.

So, I was decided. None of this was real.

I was just dreaming.

In dreams, you can do anything.

But the spider-monster in front of me is very much real. As real as can be in a dream. Because all this is just a dream. Superheroes don't really exist. And neither do spider-monsters or slime-monsters.

Avoiding the many teeth of the mutant, I successfully stab the last of its many eyes with a fire hydrant I pulled out of the ground.

The spider squeals even louder as water juts from the ground, showering the street corner. This time the arachnid attracts much more than the stare from the slime-monster. A half dozen helicopter lights beam down on us. I see the fox girl trying to signal them away and out of danger. But I doubt they will listen or understand her gestures. Even after the last explosion, the action down here is much too interesting to leave.

Final conclusion: I'll definitely be on the news. The news broadcast in my dreams, of course. Because this isn't real.

I watch the fox girl while the spider pushes into side buildings, blinded and in pain. It's snapping its teeth furiously. I suppose it's trying to get me, but I'm hovering out of range right above it. This gives me the opportunity to observe the other girl that I've nicknamed "fox girl" due to her disguise: white and rusty orange. She really looks like a fox. I wonder what I look like to her. But I will never know. And why should I care? After all, I'm the hero of this dream. I probably look much better than her, more badass.

The thought fades away when I notice it. Her arm is bleeding.

A lot.

She isn't fighting, and she's hardly defending herself. How could she have gotten so hurt? I can feel my heart pulsing in my chest, pounding faster as I hear the blood drip from Fox girl's fingertips.

All the sounds, the real sounds, suddenly kick in louder than they've ever been. The brick blocks of the establishments collapsing on the street by the impact of the blinded giant spider, the burning remnants of the chopper, and the helicopters' rotor blades … all these sounds suddenly come to focus, and the images brighten my vision, scratch away at my consciousness.

All this is now very real.

I've awoken from a dream to find that it was in fact reality.

The people in the choppers in danger of another unexpected attack, the blood seeping from Fox girl's arm, how she could lose her life, the existence of mysterious creatures … It's not just a dream. I didn't faint in the girl's bathroom and fantasized I was a superhero. The illusion is clearly gone.

I *am* a superhero.

Reality strikes me in the face. I can't describe how I feel, except for total shock. How else am I supposed to respond? Have I been this way forever: hiding alien powers deep within me? Should I be concerned? Is Fox girl the same way? Why is she handling it so well? Has she been that way for long, or did she make this new discovery recently?

I can't seem to concentrate on anything else. There are too many questions bobbling in my mind. But the helicopter beams lock on me without warning, and I am put under pressure. The world must be expecting something from me that shock prevents me from providing at the moment. I'm just sixteen years old! I'm not ready to have the weight of the world on my shoulders!

I shiver from the sweat beads on my back and tremble in dread at the scene. I force myself to recall my lonely nights in the sky, discovering flight maneuvers and I have to wonder, why *me*?

Why *us*?

I'm not alone in this crazy adventure. Fox girl seems to have relatively hit the same jackpot as me. So, what are we supposed to do about it? Am I supposed to make her my ally? Should we reveal our identities to each other? Or are we enemies?

I watch Fox girl as all these questions pester me. The slime monster launches its arms at her, appearing to be constantly swaying as though it's made of elastic bands. Whatever it's doing, it's confusing Fox girl. She doesn't seem to know what to do.

Fox girl runs to meet her opponent's palms but lets herself fall and slide forward. She successfully manages to avoid the attack. The creature is startled, or I assume it is. Its arms are not stopping their trajectory. And the guck monster simply glares at Fox girl. She, in turn, slips her foot under a wheel tire. She sends it soaring into the air. It spins uncontrollably until it reaches my height, then gravity gets a hold of it.

Below, the creature has not torn its stare from Fox girl. I'm nervous about what will happen next. Surely it won't be the end for her? I wish I knew what she had meant to do with the tire.

But then I find out.

It descends rapidly and lands ... right around the mud creature, sealing it in its grip. The extended arms fall limp.

Shouts of victory come from above. The people in the choppers are celebrating. But why? It's not over.

I look back at Fox girl and expect the creature to react. But it's gone. Fox girl must have been distracted by the shouts as well, because she looks just as astonished when she discovers the monster disappeared. I watch her face as she searches the ground for something. And I see what it is: the mud creature slips away into one of the street cracks.

Now she's looking at me. Without speaking, I know she must be waiting for me to finish up with the giant spider. But I'm not sure how to do it. I'm resisting the impulse to run away (or fly away) because now the lights of the helicopters have found me again. They must all be waiting for another heroic ending. I picture them all sitting on the edge of the seats. The rest of the world must be looking on.

Fox girl didn't disappoint them.

No pressure.

The spider is now right below me. Its snapping fangs are inches from my feet. I move away quickly, my heart clenching for a few seconds. A bit more, and I would have been a goner.

How did it get so close? But I know how it did, before the question fully forms in my thoughts. While I was looking away, it stopped squirming and tearing the buildings down. It ended the screeching cries. It came after my scent, my aura, like a quiet predator on a hunt.

I take a long breath before I swallow my fear. I was doing fine earlier, so I can do it again. I have to try, at least. But I feel like a gigantic, indestructible brick wall is in front of me – paralyzing anxiety where my mind is reeling in all the scenarios that end very badly for me, the way my family will feel when I never come home, and the repercussions of this monster-spider thing wins over me.

The one with the snapping, sharp fangs, and the salivating, dark hole that is its mouth. That's where I'll be if I can't do anything … if I don't move right now! The many bleeding eyeholes I've punched earlier are now staring right at me, threatening revenge. I'm frozen. I can't feel anything in my arms and legs. My eyes are locked on the dim opening that is my doom headed right for me. It knows where I am. Closer and closer it comes. Where is my strength? And why can't my heart stop beating so loud? The wind whistles through my hair, as though trying to aid me in movement. But the cold reality says I'm about to be devoured.

    I take in a long breath.

8

VENOM

There's a part of my youth I just can't remember. My memories date back to when I was around twelve years old. Everything before that is locked away, sealed in the darkness of my mind. I suspect foul play in my youth, and troubling events. Why else would my mind repress twelve years of innocence?

The only lingering recollection still available to my consciousness is the lack of air in my lungs, my breath too short to catch, burning my throat. The sun blinds me, but still I run. Faster and faster, I go. My shirt is drenched and sticks to my sweaty skin. My shoelaces are detached, swaying wildly from side to side. I need to make it. I need to get home. But I'm lost.

Whatever I was running from, it must have been scary. But now I don't have to run. No more running away from scary things. I can defend myself. This giant spider, or any other creature that will cross my path or hurt the innocent, shall find their doom. There is nothing that can stop me now. As I allow myself to swallow these words as my own, as I allow myself to embrace my situation and my secret identity, I also realize that there are so many more things to think about.

What was I created for?

What is my purpose?

Who can I trust?

Who is my enemy?

What do they want?

How will I defeat such a threat?

Who or what is their target?

Where are all these creatures coming from?

Is it the end of the world?

Without warning, the giant spider swallows the space between its teeth and me. My heart silences and my eyes lose focus, releasing all sounds and the surroundings. The world seems alive again, rushing back to me at light speed.

I reach forward and grip one of the spider's many snapping teeth. The hard chelicera slices my palms slightly. My warm blood drips instantly into the dark mouth below me, exciting the spider for more. The creature tries to pull away in order to thrust forward with more vigor, but instead it finds that my grasp is more powerful than its brute resistance.

I am amazed at my sharp reflexes, my instincts, and my strength. I didn't know I was capable of acting so quickly. My body had already clasped the tooth before the thought crossed my mind. Everything is faster, stronger, and better with this new body, with this new Dana.

The spider keeps yanking, trying to break free. At last, I pull on the tooth only to find it firmly attached. But a squeal from the creature and a tear in the tooth divulges a weakness.

I've inflicted pain.

The spider, now far more desperate, jerks harder, its legs finding fortitude on the partly demolished buildings and on the severed street.

I see what happens next before it does. A thrill fills my body with anticipation. I tug on the fang and it finally breaks loose.

The spider and I both pause for a moment. I'm faster than the creature at realizing what comes next. It only takes me seconds to find shelter higher up in the air from a furious and spiteful creature. Its bestial aggressiveness against the buildings serves only to send the towers crumbling down.

The blocks fall on top of the large hairy body. I watch the creature get buried from high above it and take some distance from the rubble and dust. I hold my breath because I feel like everyone watching is doing the same. The dusty cloud clears away, and I wait.

I know it's not over. I feel it.

I loosen my grip on my prize, thinking the numbness in my fingers is because I'm holding it too tightly. As I take a look at my hand, I succumb to another type of paralysis. This shock resonates in my entire body and frightens me to death. My heart is in overdrive. My stomach churns. I begin to hyperventilate and shake uncontrollably.

A purple liquid seeps from the top of the broken tooth to my hand. My severed hand.

Venom.

My first instinct is to release the fang, but instead I hold it even tighter. A thought crosses my mind: maybe my new body rejects this poison, and it will have no effect on me. It's a less than probable scenario, but I'm hopeful.

"Are you okay?"

The voice startles me. Fox girl is levitating near me, careful to keep her distance. Her face is paler than earlier. The blood is still dripping from her fingers.

"Are you okay?" she repeats.

She's bleeding to death and yet worries for my safety. Why is she so concerned? Perhaps she feels a connection with me. Perhaps she wants to form an alliance. Perhaps she needs to know if I'm friend or foe.

"Do you need help?" she asks me.

"No," I bluntly retort.

Fox girl seems taken aback. But I didn't mean it that way. I cringe from the sudden pain running through my arm. The veins in my hand look like purple snakes, darker at my wound, crawling to my forearm.

Fox girl sees what has gotten my attention. She approaches carefully until she's at arm's length from me.

"It seems we're both in need of medical attention," she says. Her tone says it all: pain is harder to hide in her voice. Her grasp on her arm tightens.

"Yeah," I agree. I can feel the poison sliding up my arm, shocking my shoulder and my neck. The agony is unbearable. "Obviously, we need help! You're probably as new to this as I am."

I'm very rude. I know that. But what she said was so *duh*. Stupid comments deserve stupid answers.

Fox girl stares at me and stays quiet for the next few minutes. Her arm is completely limp now. The purple venom has finally spread to my neck. It's getting harder to breathe.

"Let's start over," she says. Her voice is low now. But she seems determined to stay right here. "My name's K-"

Fox girl cuts her sentence short. Either the pain has gotten to her, or she forgot her name. I realize that if she asks me my name, I won't know what to say. My heart should be racing, and I should be nervous. But my heart slows down, and the world is almost quiet. It strikes me that the poison must have reached my ear and is headed straight for my brain and heart. I must make a decision right NOW.

Either I leave the spider there, alive under the rubble, and let it destroy the rest of the city. Or I stay, finish it off, and most likely die here with K-.

"Kitsune," Fox girl finally blurts out.

"What?" I ask her, unsure if I heard right, or if I was *really* going deaf. "Can't you see this is a *very* bad time for introductions?" I must have said all that louder than expected due to my affected hearing.

"Okay," she responds. "I'm leaving." She turns and slowly starts for what I guess is the nearest hospital.

'We're both going to die,' I think.

Kitsune once again tries to fly away, but her body descends toward the ground.

The helicopter lights are on her. She barely makes it to the ground when her body gives up. Kitsune falls the last few meters to the street. She is completely wilted, her torso hanging in the crevice in the cement. Her arms are suspended over her head. The blood is still trickling down her fingers.

That's how I'll be in a few minutes.

Dead.

It's too late for me now. I have no more energy. There's nothing left in me. My hearing ability is gone. All I can hear are my own thoughts reflecting my imminent death. My heart is slow enough to make me dizzy. The pain is so intense I barely feel it now.

The wreckage trembles below. There it is. I knew it couldn't be over. The building blocks jet in all directions. The spider tears from its prison and comes straight for me.

With everything left in me, I instinctively rush to spear the creature with its own weapon. I pressure the venomous tooth in the spider's head. It jerks away, squeals loudly enough for me to hear, and permanently succumbs. The corpse dries up, the legs curl, and the spider rolls on its back.

Now it's my turn. My body is surrendering to nature. My head spins. The lights dissolve.

9
INSTINCTS

The shadow of a bird passes over my head on the pavement, and I watch it as it makes circles and disappears. I look up and find the bird perched on the roof, completely ignoring the crowd below. Right now, I wish I could fly off, but instead I'm glued to the ground. I wonder how so much of nature can be free and I feel imprisoned inside myself.

Since I woke up this morning, questions have been jostling within me, and even if I scratch my memory, nothing sparks. I'm left completely in the dark about what happened that night after I killed the spider creature. That was a week ago.

A part of me doesn't believe it really happened, and at moments, I almost fall back into my fantasy state where nothing is real and all is a dream. But constant reminders keep me in check: the news broadcast, the pictures of Kitsune and I in the paper, and our silhouettes on billboards. Overnight, we became important.

We became *real* superheroes.

Both admired and hated, Kitsune and I were what everyone was talking about. And with all that, you'd think someone knew what happened to us when the fight was over. But no one knows. The story ends when I fall, the helicopter lights go out, and Kitsune and I vanish. In the morning, I wake up in my bed, rested and energized.

I look down at my hand, the one that was plagued with spider venom. There was no trace left of the poison except for the gash in my hand turned purple. It was still healing while my other hand showed no marker of a wound. Perhaps my venom-infested hand might never truly heal, but for now, I keep the injury away from anyone's eyes.

So far, it's been successful. This year has been colder than usual, even in this month of September. So I've heard. The cold no longer has any effect on me, so I rely on people's complaints. I've started wearing sweaters with sleeves long enough to cover my palms. Sometimes I even recur to thin gloves. During warmer days, I keep my hands in my pockets, or on my bag handle. Although not everyone wears a sweater on windy days, Kass seems to always wear one no matter the weather. She seems very fragile lately.

The students shuffle to get inside the theatre. I try to stay close to Kass and Brydhen while keeping an eye out for the others: Richard, Seleste and Scotty, my new friends.

Scotty is the boy from math class who sits beside me. His style still has not improved, even to this day. He continues to embarrass himself publicly in his baggy jeans with a pit bulldog sticker on the back pocket and a neon blue thick cotton sweatshirt. I catch his eyes for only a brief moment until he diverts his gaze. I'm not sure what kind of stare, nor with what kind of eyes he looks at me. Is it timidity or is it love? It can't be love because he barely knows me. He behaves the same way in math and ethics class. In both cases, I sit next to Scotty and in front of Brydhen. Only in gym class do I avoid both boys altogether: Brydhen because he pays much more attention to what he's asked to do, and Scotty because he doesn't have gym class.

The thing about gym is that I have to be careful. I don't yet know how to control my strength and power. I'm mostly afraid of hitting a ball too hard, jumping too high or running faster and for longer than everyone. I need to be within the average for a girl my age. So, I imitate other girls: pretend to be lazy and unmotivated for sport, let alone exercise.

We're asked for our tickets once we cross the threshold. I hand mine over to a middle-aged man dress in a black and white formal suit. He looks displeased and gives me the impression that he hates me. Or it's a general distaste for teenagers.

Then I see it. Right behind his head is a poster of Kitsune and I. It's a collage of the other night: Kitsune drifting on the street, reaching for the tire with her foot; and me, yanking on the spider tooth. It looks great with the starry night and the helicopter beams.

Very impressive.

Every time I envision that night, a chill runs through me. Perhaps it is due to remembering the pain I was in, and the fantasy I was pulled out of. It could also be caused from the tickling in my hand where the poison infiltrated my bloodstream. It is still a mystery to me.

The strangest thing about that night was the lack of assistance. Why was it all up to Kitsune and I to rid the city of alien creatures? Why wasn't the military present? Or even the police, for that matter? That's what happens in movies ... So why didn't they help us?

I am motioned into a semi-lit aisle, left to find my seat number on my own. I reach my chair positioned to the right side of the stage, almost in the middle of the hall. I sit on the comfortable, red duvet cushion and scan the chamber. There were four emergency exit doors, and the main entrances were at the back. The double doors were grand - large enough to fit a crowd.

While I wait for my fellow classmates and other students to fill the theatre, I think back on the first time I spoke with Scotty. It was two days ago at lunch break. I was supposed to meet Kass in the dining hall, but I was sidetracked. I saw him sitting alone, which was a surprise because he was never alone. He was always surrounded with dozens of people at a time. I cautiously approached, just enough to see why he was leaning over the table. He looked like a child: legs crossed on the bench, elbows on the table supporting his weight, and his attention completely focused on a chart.

It was a map of the stars and planets in our solar system.

"Makes us feel small, doesn't it?" I said to him. But he didn't look up. He probably didn't hear me. So, I sat down in front of him and repeated my question.

This time he noticed me. His face blushed the same way it always did when he saw me. He nodded in response. Then we spent the next hour lost in space. He told me which planets we could see at certain times of the year, what stars were, and where astrological signs could be found. Kass joined us after half an hour. She didn't ask where I had been, and that was alright with me. She seemed just as interested by Scotty's lecture. Brydhen stood behind Kass and I, silent as usual.

To this day, Brydhen's presence is intoxicating to me. And exhausting. My breaths are shorter, my heart thumps harder, and anxiety simmers in the pit of my stomach every time he's around. Even if I don't believe it, and even if I want to ignore the feelings, they are there. Brydhen is there. His essence is buried in every one of my thoughts.

"Dana!" I hear behind me. I turn and find Kass sitting two seats away. "I lost Brydhen on my way, but Richard is right there," she says, pointing three seats to my left.

He looked over at me and smiled, waving his hand idiotically. "What's this play about again?" he asks.

"Doubt, treason, and death," I reply thoughtfully, by my understanding of Hamlet.

Richard keeps smiling awkwardly as if it's frozen on his face, but he's clearly lost in thought. Even sitting, Richard is tall and skinny. His long, raven hair, black pinch, and dark eyes are all part of the clown appearance he's extruding. His face projects maturity, his hair rebellion, and his behaviour infancy. But I like that about him. He's different.

When Kass and I met Richard, moments after we neared Scotty, he introduced us to Seleste Jones. Seleste, tall, short brown hair always tied in a ponytail, and blue eyes, remains a mystery to me, even if I speak with her in French class all the time. During breaks, she reads or does homework. But she barely speaks unless spoken to first.

Richard is the contrary. He speaks too much. He expresses himself through grand hand gestures, the kind that makes you keep some distance to avoid all unnecessary injuries.

In one day, three people entered my life and I feel the need to find out more about them. I'm happy my little gang of three is expanding, but it's hard to get to know them. It's like there isn't enough hours in a day to speak to everyone, ask all the right questions, and label someone as friend. Although Richard, Scotty and Seleste have brought more life in the gang, it has slightly pushed Brydhen away. He barely says a word, and his stare isn't as deep and penetrating. Something changed for him, and I intend to find out what it is.

The lights begin to dim, calling everyone's attention to the stage almost immediately. Everything goes silent. I expect to hear some shuffling on the stage when the actors take their spots, but I hear nothing. In seconds, my vision adjusts to the darkness. I look around me, astonished. I can see everything so clearly! Just like in the movies, night vision allows to see in shades of green. My eyes have imitated this ability. I smile, content and impressed. Who knew that I would have everything necessary to be powerful? To be invincible. To be nothing close to human.

And then a feeling takes over me. It reminds me of anxiety but multiplied times ten. My stomach cramps and hurts. It's very uncomfortable. I squirm uneasily in my seat, knowing very well that there's something wrong. There's something *terribly* wrong.

10

RIPPED

I'm glued to my chair, dumbfounded by what I see. The floorboards of the stage rise as though a balloon is growing underneath. The wood cracks and complains from stretching and expanding. The spectators whisper and cough, puzzled by the never-ending darkness of the room. It rends every person here vulnerable. But not me.

A deafening noise makes everyone feel uneasy. They toss in their seats, awaiting any kind of comfort. The grand doors at the back of the theatre bolt, and the emergency door signs turn off, stealing away the faint light they provided. Darkness and agitation overtake the chamber instantly.

The center stage explodes. Floorboards burst into the air. People start to rise. The ones sitting at the front immediately evacuate their spots. They blindly stumble in the aisle and successfully manage to reach the back of the room. Others imitate their behaviour although they cannot see what people are doing while staggering each other's feet. Most are poised to their seats, confused but patient.

So far, nothing very life-threatening is taking place. But it's hard to define any danger when people assemble in the aisle, concealing the most important part of the stage. A few of them reach the exit and try to pry the doors open with no luck. A couple of people help, but the doors don't budge. Soon, a dozen people attempt the impossible.

Noises that I can only describe as excited evil children with hoarse voices fill the room. Everyone goes silent, and all heads turn to the stage. The line of students in the aisle obscures my vision. But I don't need to see anything to know that it's not the actors starting the play.

I stand up and focus on trying to see what's happening on the stage. Like my eyes knew how all along, they focus on exactly what I want. The bodies in the way become translucent, and the smaller forms, the ones rising from the hole in the stage, become well defined.

They're little monsters looking at the crowd with hungry faces. I can only imagine that for them, they see a chamber full of fresh meat ready to be served. They're barely taller than five-year olds. Their heads are larger and rounder than their bodies, their ears spiky and excessively big, and their skin is like scales. They all have long beards, and wide, glowing eyes that I guess allow them to see in darkness. They look very hungry and thrilled with excitement upon the sight of defenseless prey.

But they're not defenseless. Not if I can help it.

Now is the perfect time to revisit a good friend. But I can't do it in front of everyone. We may be in total darkness, but the last time I transformed (which is how I'll call it), there were glowing golden rings around me. I can't take the chance that it will happen again. Everyone will see.

I look around me. Richard is at the back doors, and Kass is gone. I'm guessing she's at the exit too. I turn to the stage again and find that the creatures have slowly started to creep toward the crowd, descending one by one from the steps. Then I spot my perfect hideout: the curtains at the front. They are thick enough to hide any light emanating from me. I run to the end of the row and to the heavy velvet curtains. I pull them quickly around my body and make sure I'm completely surrounded.

I pause.

I don't know how to transform. The last time was extremely painful and out of my control. I didn't choose for that to happen. So how do I do it now?

My heart pulses hard, and my stomach churns. It makes me feel weak and powerless. But I have to figure out how to change. It will conceal my identity and allow me some freedom. No inhibitions. But how? How!

I peak from behind the curtain and observe the crowd of students panicking. Kassidy and others, lost in the frenzy, have completely disappeared.

Although I took only a few seconds to notice this, it was time enough to be spotted. One of the creatures stares me down and waits for a reaction. It's standing, breathless and salivating, approximately five meters away. Its eyes are mesmerizing, glowing and bright, locked on my position. Its sharpened claws and savage thrill to kill are very obvious. The creature takes a step forward... then another. Still, I offer no reaction, no apparent understanding that its presence means immediate danger. The creature takes another breath, heavy and intense. My luck runs out. It decides it's going for it. I have now become a lucky treat ready for the taking.

I gulp as I watch the creature run to me. I back away into the corner, trapped. There's nowhere for me to go. I'm done for if I can't transform!

The creature lunges. I gasp. My heart stops. I'm so scared my body freezes. I shut my eyes and hope for a miracle.

The darkness of my eyelids is suddenly lit with gold.

I feel it.

I feel the change happening.

But what about the creature? I crack open an eye to venture a look. The creature, now on the floor, is a mess of blood and guts - split down the middle, but vertically from head to toe.

I instantly gag.

The damage must have been done during the transformation. The power of the gold rings must have cut clean through the creature's body, protecting me at a vulnerable time.

The creature never stood a chance.

I realize now that my hands are shaking and wet. I cling to the curtain and pull it toward me. Peering over at the stage, I hear a disturbance.

Kitsune, she's here!

Why does she always appear where I am? Does she have a danger sensor? More to the point, how did she get here so fast?

Unless … she was here already!

The thought vanishes when I notice that more creatures have spotted me. But it's time to unveil myself. I leap and land dead center of the stage, to the right of the creature-infested hole. Quickly I learn that the little brutes are agile and vicious. The closest one to me digs its claws into my stomach to earn a firm grip. The pain shoots through me like lightning. I'm blinded and unable to move or scream. I can't see what rips through my pants and bites into my leg. I feel my stomach getting cold, and yet, the skin underneath is warm and humid. I hold in the biggest scream of my life, but the tears are unstoppable. Instinctively, and I suppose very consciously, I reach for the creature on my stomach, the one smiling at me, and fiercely pull it off, along with a large amount of skin.

"AHHH," I bellow. All I want to do is cry, yell, and hit something. That hurt like hell. Every part of me burns, and my stomach is frozen and simultaneously burning hot. The pain transfers to my leg. Both my hands are busy holding the first creature at bay. I torpedo the thing upward and through the ceiling. The light of the sun instantly pours down on me. The monster clenching my leg releases my flesh and scampers angrily for darkness.

"So … light hurts you," I breathe through gritted teeth.

Screams and gasps of horror catch my attention. The crowd of students can finally see what has them panicked. And it has them panicked even more. Now their yells and fear attract the little demons.

Like predators, the monsters slowly advance as a group toward their prey. Kitsune and I are no longer exciting. I look over at her for advice, but her glare does not cross mine. She continues to stare at the creatures as though trying to figure something out. Then her face diverts to the ceiling.

I get a bad feeling about her plan.

My stomach and leg have me pinned to the stage, the blood rushing through the lesions. And then I figure it out. If that girl thinks of bathing the theatre in sunshine, the creatures will run for what darkness is left: exactly where the students are standing.

Ripped by pain but afraid for my friends, I fly over to the crowd and try to push my way through. I hear the words 'coward' and 'hero,' but I ignore them.

"MOVE!" I yell, and some students let me through to the doors. Blood is oozing down my stomach, crusting around my belt, staining my pants. My leg is stinging and sending painful electrical bolts to my knee and foot. I feel like my leg will soon surrender to my weight and abandon all hope. Despite this, I try to push open the grand doors.

I'm faced with resistance, but not a 'bolted-lock' kind of resistance. I'm looking at, as unbelievable as it seems, a powerful 'you-will-not-open-these-doors-because-of-my-magic' kind of resistance. The doors are not locked at all, but something is evidently holding them closed.

"We already tried that," says a person next to me. He is obviously referring to pushing the doors open, and not the insane idea of a magic spell at work going through my mind at the moment.

"Yes, well … you don't have my powers," I retort. I find that speaking, let alone standing, is harder than I think. Pain shoots through me every time I make a basic movement, like lifting a finger. I want to push the doors again, just to make sure, but I know it won't work. The doors won't budge just because I try again, or because I will them to. It will take more than that. It will take something I don't have.

A bright light suddenly fills the room. I glance over my shoulder and see that the stage no longer has a roof. Kitsune has torn it apart. And just as I suspected, the little monsters chase after the safety of darkness. They're running straight for us.

I raise both my palms and push the doors as hard as I can, all-the-while my vision returns to normal. I try again a little harder, but nothing happens. The pain on my stomach makes me dizzy and weak. I feel like if I try anything else, my body will shut down instantly. No one will be saved.

Right now, I'm thinking Kitsune means well, but she's really stupid. She's jeopardizing everyone's life. What the hell is she thinking? And how am I going to get these people out of here without crashing?

More light vibrates in the hall. It's time I do something. Kitsune obviously does not see the problem! So, I ignore the pain, my stomach, my leg, my spinning head, and I push the doors again, and again, and again …

"They're almost on us!" someone shouts.

My heart beats faster. I'm so nervous and dizzy I have to shut my eyes. "You better open," I threaten. As a last effort, I take two steps back and fling myself against the doors.

They burst open.

Not a second later, students are pushing past me.

I give in to the enormous amount of pain searing through me. The burning sensation on my stomach and the feeling of my pulse in my leg disappears from my mind. I can't open my eyes. I've dropped to my knees while the warmth of the sun engulfs me. I force my eyelids open just in time to see a few creatures trying to lunge through the grand doors, but the sunrays reach them first. They disintegrate in mid-plunge.

My eyes close again. I take a few breaths, wondering if it's all downhill from here. Was I really made to be a superhero? Was all of this a test and I failed? Will I live to see another day?

I feel a warm hand touch mine. Then a grip around my wrist and my arm being lifted, tugged behind someone's neck. And my limp body is raised off the floor.

"You're going to be okay," a girl's voice says in my ear. At first, it sounded like Kass. But then I really hoped it wasn't. If it is, that means she's still here and I wasn't able to save her. Maybe it's someone else, an angel in heaven. I find the strength, or I think it was mostly curiosity, to peak at my saviour.

It's Kitsune!

"What were you thinking?" I manage to spit out.

"What do you mean?" she responds, puzzlement in her voice.

"You threatened the lives of everyone," I tell her, as though it was the most obvious thing on earth.

"Nah, I knew you'd open the doors in time. I had faith in you," she says.

I register that my body is quickly turning cold. The warmth of the sun is gone. Everything in my head is spinning wildly.

And then it all stops. The dizziness, the pain, the running blood – there's no more. I can finally open my eyes.

I'm flabbergasted.

I'm all healed!

There's no trace of ever having been bitten on the leg, or having skin ripped at the stomach. I'm all okay!

I peer at my left hand, the one that had been scarred by the giant spider and infected with venom. Unfortunately, my luck has to run out somewhere.

The scar is still there, and strongly apparent. I feel like it's never going to heal, and instead become a part of me.

"How …" I mutter. My question is rather simple until I realize I'm nowhere near the theatre now. The room I'm in is not as grand, and entirely made of metal. There's a giant screen along the far wall. To my right is a domed wall, as though the room behind is circular. Everything else is plain and lifeless.

I feel so confused. One moment I was in the theatre feeling the life drain from me. Everything spins in circles, and I think death is knocking at my door. But when I open my eyes, here I am: all healed in a prison-like chamber with no clue as to how I got here, or where 'here' is.

Kitsune, just as clueless, releases me and articulates my thought exactly. "Where are we?"

KASSIDY

11

ALCIDOR

Everything is happening way too fast. Dana doesn't seem to be as fazed by it as much as post people. First, there was an attack downtown. There I was, in complete shock, fighting a mud-monster with a face – and as unbelievable as it was – with a voice. Despite the fact that I was more concerned with how astonishingly instinctual it was to fight Predzellmoo, I got hurt. Really badly hurt.

All I remember was passing out after trying to make a connection with the other fighter. I know it was stupid and definitely not the time – as she crudely remarked – but I felt a connection there.

Silly me, I almost gave away my actual name, Kassidy. But lucky me, I found another name that started with the letter 'k.' The only thing that came to mind was 'kitsune,' a word that means fox in Japanese. I may have been out of it at that point, but some mental neurons were still firing, enough to give my alter ego a name.

It's faint, but I also remember the other fighter having a cut on her left hand – a really bad one. The venom was turning purple in her blood stream, and quickly spreading up her arm. How she survived that is beyond me.

Where this whole thing gets seriously messed up is when the goblins attacked the theatre. Loads of things still bother me about it. It seems strange to me that the attack at the theatre just happened to be when I was there. Second, where the other fighter also happened to be. Coincidence, I think not. That connection that I felt to her seems a lot more relevant now, but it has me wondering if she was already at the theatre, or she had come on the school fieldtrip, which would mean that she was a student in my grade, and at my school.

What's also interesting are the creatures that are attacking the city. They all seem to be coming from the ground. Some of them are familiar, like the giant spider, while others, like Predzellmoo and the goblins, are right out of horror stories. Like aliens, almost. But that can't be, right? Aliens don't exist.

Aliens don't exist, I repeat to myself as I look around the room. A moment ago, we were in the theatre, and I was wondering how I was going to help the other fighter. But now she's all healed. She looks just as stupid as I probably look. Clearly, neither one of us understands how we got here.

"Where are we?" I ask, knowing full well that she wouldn't know either.

I notice the exit doors almost right away. It's mostly a reflex, in case this is a trap. There are two, both to my right. One is behind me; the other is at the end of the room beside a giant screen. They don't look like regular doors; rather, they look like sliding doors, divided down the middle. They merge so well with the room by their colour and texture that anyone else without my awesome eyes would maybe not see them.

The room is pretty big, but uniform in colour. It's a shade of depressing gray, like a snowy scene in a black and white movie. The rest of the room is bare. The large screen in front is on, and it's displaying DNA strings beside two female bodies. The strings repeatedly couple with a strange DNA code to create significant changes in the two female bodies.

But something particular catches my attention. In front of the gigantic screen is a small shadow with neon green eyes. In fact, it looks a lot like a Halloween prop, an otherworldly creature just standing there to scare us. But it doesn't scare me. The miniature, grey thing wears a black, leather coat over its shoulders and owns six, small arms. The creature looks so *real*.

"Hello," I hear. It's a male voice for sure. I look around the room quickly for anyone else. But other than the other fighter and I, the room is quite literally empty.

"Who said that?" she says to the room in general. But no one answers. The room is silent. Maybe it was an invisible being. How surprising would that be? Or a voice over speakers.

"Down here," the voice says. My eyes dart back to the Halloween prop. I can't quite describe the way the slithery and strong voice sent shivers up my spine. What I heard is definitely not human.

I feel my heart thump hard against my chest, and the butterflies fly wildly in my gut.

Aliens don't exist, I tell myself again.

I look to my left at the other girl. Her stare is blank, and her mouth is slightly open. She lifts her arm and points directly at the alien Halloween prop.

I shake my head because every cell in my body refuses to believe it.

"It's okay to be shocked. You've never seen someone like me before," the alien says.

I see its mouth moving, the twitch of an arm when it said, 'someone like me,' and yet, my mind refuses to accept it. An alien. Not a Halloween prop. An alien. Six arms. Neon eyes. Big eyes.

That's a 'no' from my brain. Just an absolute 'no.'

"Come. You will adjust. We have not a lot of time. I must show you something."

Still in shock, I approach it carefully. It was an automatic reflex – to do as I'm told.

I look over my shoulder at the other girl. She relaxed her arm and closed her mouth, but her face is still blank. She's obviously as confused and stupefied as I am. She hasn't moved any closer like I have, and I think maybe that's wise. I should probably keep my distance too. So, I take two steps back quietly and look up at the bright screen.

The alien turns its back to me and points to the screen. An image suddenly appears. It's a perfect replica of the other girl's body and mine at two different ends of the screen. Our bodies are spinning slowly like ballet dancer dolls in a jewelry box. Between the images of us were four different DNA scrolls. From left to right, they read *Original DNA*, *Dragon DNA*, *Fox DNA*, and *Original DNA*. I watch closely as the DNA scrolls on the screen bond and create two unique blends, dragon-human and fox-human.

I don't understand a single thing. Millions of questions (and I guess, a philosophical debate on being alone in the universe, too) are drowning all common sense and my ability to integrate new information.

"Who are you?" I mutter, still unable to believe I'm speaking to an alien, and not a Halloween prop. A part of my brain is laughing at me for talking to a Halloween prop and actually trying to accept the words it will tell me as the ultimate truth.

"My name is Alcidor," it answers.

My mind is rushing. All the movies about aliens, the stereotypes created to someday help us be prepared and believe, are all coming back to me. But none of them suffice to help me accept this. It's just too unreal!

"*What* are you?" The sound of the other girl's voice confirms how I feel. It's comforting to know that I'm not the only one facing this unbelievable trauma.

"All answers will come in due time," it says flatly, never turning to look at us.

"So, then what are we doing here?" I ask. There's reproach in my voice. "And where's *here*?"

Alcidor finally turns to face us. "Listen, and listen carefully. This is important."

Another moment of silence keeps us hanging for answers.

The tone of his voice dropped. "We do not have a lot of time. Before you return, you must understand who you are and what you must do. Who and what I am does not yet have importance," he says.

Everything is even stranger than before. I have more questions than answers. The suspense is making it worse. Not being able to think straight while these questions poke at me is making me nervous.

"First, the lightning bolt was no accident. It was the only way I could alter your DNA without suspicion. Like you see behind me, one of you has fox and the other dragon DNA."

"You did *what*?" the girl exclaims. It sounded a lot like an accusation. And I can't really blame her. A lightning bolt that could have killed us changed our basic DNA, mixed it with an animal's, for what?

"Get used to it, Dragoon. It is only beginning," Alcidor orders, dismissing the girl's outrage.

"Dragoon?" she says, instead.

"Yes, that is your name. And you," he says while turning to me. I gulp my life away. "I had a better name for you. But you have chosen an appropriate one."

"You two were the only ones whose DNA could be altered without damage, and your convictions were perfect for the job," Alcidor continues.

"Dragons don't exist," Dragoon interrupts again.

"Neither do superheroes or aliens," Alcidor retorts, glancing quickly my way. A warning bell in my head goes off. Can the alien hear what I'm thinking? Because moments ago, I was trying to convince myself that aliens don't exist.

I almost want to laugh, but the awkwardness of the situation keeps me quiet. I'm still trying to listen to an alien all the while trying to get passed the fact that it's an alien.

"What do you mean we're the only ones?" The question forms out loud before I can stop it. Alcidor's eyes fall on me, and for a second there, my throat tightens, and I hold my breath, afraid of the alien's reaction. But Alcidor doesn't react.

"Your human DNA is unique. You have a special kind of chromosome that allows for change to occur without major physical or intellectual detriments. There are very few of you among billions, and so I had to ensure you were moved to the same location as our enemy.

"My species has been trying to defend our planet from our neighbours," Alcidor continues. "In your language, they are called *witches*. My species and the witches are both immortal, but their planet can no longer hold its inhabitants. They sought to take over our planet but failed. For over one thousand human years, my species has resisted the witches. Now they have discovered the next habitable planet where its natives would never be able to protect themselves from an invasion. Earth.

"Not even your military prowess stands a chance against them. They sent one witch to annihilate everyone on Earth, beginning with the primary source of life that they don't need, but you do: water. It only took one drop of a very powerful potion to make water transform to worms. First, the small streams will be affected; second, the rivers, lakes, seas, and last of all, oceans. Everything will fall to her mercy. In about four years from now, there will be no water left. All the animals on Earth will die, spreading disease and exterminating humans forever."

Alcidor pauses. Good thing too because I feel like I'm going to vomit. All life on Earth… gone. In four years! That's not fair! That's not enough time. I've never even fallen in love, or really lived. Why is this happening to us?

He continues. My heart churns. "This is where you come in. While this is happening, you will have to fight back while we arrange a planet-wide evacuation. There is no way to reverse the transformation of the water, so you will have to bring the survivors of Earth to another planet. Earth is lost forever."

My heart drops. My mind reals with questions or scenarios where we can still save the earth. But Alcidor used the present tense, 'is lost,' like it's already too late.

I try to process the information, but it seems so unreal. It's so hard to believe. It feels like a really bad dream, or an apocalyptical movie starring two teenagers who have no idea what they're doing. And on top of that, a global evac? How will we pull this off? Our species can barely build rockets that hold more than its astronauts. And then Alcidor's words hit me.

"I thought you said the only other habitable planet is Earth?" I whisper.

"For the witches, yes. But they cannot breathe with oxygen, nor can they live on a cool planet like Earth. They will have to completely or drastically destroy the ozone lawyer and change the atmosphere. Earth is well on its way to its end by the human's destructive nature. There are other planets - newer, younger. The witches would die there. Here, they have a fighting chance," Alcidor explains.

"The witch most likely contacted her species already, and surely, they are on their way here as we speak. It will take them four years to arrive," he says, as though it was supposed to be comforting. "Now that you understand your fate, you must seek out the witch. Work together and find her. Go!"

12

PLANNING

A lot of things are still unclear. Where were we? Where had Alcidor taken us? How did he heal Dragoon's wounds in seconds? Were there others, or was it just Dragoon and me? How was Alcidor planning to organize a global evacuation? And when? How did he plan to fit billions of people on spaceships, and convince them to leave their home planet for another world? On another note, what if Dragoon and I do find the witch? What do we do with her? Kill her? Incarcerate her? Bring her to Alcidor?

I'm sitting in Dana's basement on the floor beside her. We were supposed to watch a movie, the gang and I, but something interesting happened on TV. The President of the United States took over all Canadian channels. The live feed is informing all citizens of the weird occurrences. Apparently, our little city isn't the only one affected by strange phenomena. But compared to us, they have the military on their side. Now the army is patrolling the streets at every hour of the day, the police presence tripled, and the fire fighters and first responders are always on the move. The whole world is in need of superheroes … against strange creatures and giant, worm infestations rising from the ground. I knew that first worm we saw weeks ago wasn't a robot malfunction.

"Things like these are clearly unnatural. Something is happening to our planet that we still don't understand. Our leading scientists are exploring the matter. I advise each and every one of you to be cautious and avoid crowded spaces. This does not mean that we should cease our daily activities. Go to school, go to work, and pay your taxes. As for the water, be careful. We will do our best to clean the water supplies, but we ask you to do the same at home. Boil the water before using or buy bottled water to be sure. Above all, be safe."

We're all sitting in silence, listening to the news on TV. To the others, it's unbelievable and extraordinary. But to me, it's becoming increasingly real. There's nothing the President can say that I don't already know. In fact, I'm sure they know a lot more and the government is forced to withhold information in order to keep the peace. But I feel like it won't hold for long, not when things are going to get much worse – like Alcidor described.

So Scotty, slumped on the sofa behind me, is bored and unimpressed. Brydhen beside him, is staring blankly at the screen. At the other end of the couch, Richard is growing impatient. Dana actually looks interested. And Seleste, sitting on Dana's left, is scanning the room rather than the TV.

"They have no idea what's going on," I say, matter-of-factly, even though I'm convinced the government knows more than it's letting on. Like how the attacks are happening all over the world, and how they know about Dragoon's presence and mine in this fight, but they don't even mention us. They also don't tell us why the military and the police are completely absent from our city. Like, is it all up to Dragoon and I to defend the city?

"What was that?" Richard asks.

"Nothing…" I answer.

"No, really. What did you say?" Richard says. "Anything to concentrate on is better than a no-good broadcast."

"She said they obviously know nothing. In other words, this is a waste of time," Dana translates for me.

"I'll tell you what's more interesting. It's those girls – the ones who saved us at the theatre," Seleste says. She's been so quiet I forgot what her voice sounded like. But she hit the jackpot. Everyone always wants to talk about Dragoon and Kitsune. In classes, on the news, and online videos, it's always about us.

"It's interesting, yes. But what's strange is that they appeared at the same time that all this started happening: the water, the monsters, the attacks…" Brydhen says. Everyone is caught off guard by his idea, but his words prolong the silence. For a moment, it sounded like Brydhen was insinuating that Dragoon and Kitsune were part of the problem, or that they were somehow responsible for the attacks. But it's easy to put the blame on someone who wants to help, because you don't know what's going on and you're out of the 'know.'

"I don't think so," I say loudly, interrupting a silence that was making me feel uncomfortable. "They wouldn't have protected us from those little goblins, the spider and the mud monster … not if they were a part of all this."

And now it feels like I'm protecting my reputation among my own friends. It almost sounds like an excuse – or rather, a poor defense.

"I guess…" Richard responds, but he sounds unconvinced. "You have to admit that they sort of *showed up*."

"No one knows *anything*, so all this is just conjecture. They might be involved like they might be saving us. Who knows really, other than them?" Dana argues.

And now I feel relieved. I thought everyone would be against Dragoon and I, that we were the bad guys.

"Monsters seem to show up whenever there's an event – a *student* event. Do you think something will happen tomorrow, while we're at the convention?" Seleste asks.

She hits another jackpot. Not directly, but she does have a point. If I recall correctly, the spider and Predzellmoo's attacks occurred a block away from school. The goblin infestation during a student event at the theatre was the only thing that saved us from writing an English report, one that I refused to write with or without an attack. But back to the point: are the students a primary target? Are they related somehow to the end of the world? Or has the witch discovered that the city's superheroes are students (if indeed Dragoon is a student)?

My heart drops. If the witch knows I'm a student, if she knows who I am, does this mean that my family is in danger? I swallow my irrational fear.

"We could ask Sandra when activities take place. She knows all of them for the full year," Scotty notes, straightening in his seat. His eyes glitter like an excited child. "She follows these things. She even knows if they're cancelled."

"That's obsession," Seleste retorts, unimpressed.

"Yeah, but it works in our favour," Brydhen replies smiling. "We can attend all events and determine for ourselves if *super-one* and *super-two* are on our side."

"That's stupid," Dana responds. "You could get yourself killed. You might as well jump off a bridge." She never takes her eyes off the TV screen.

She's holding the remote control with both hands close to her chest, and keeps it pointed to the ceiling. It's as though she's bothered by Brydhen's remark, and at the same time, as though she doesn't really care.

But no one listens to her. The whole group agrees that they will attend all the scheduled events. They really don't understand the danger in that. They turn to me and pressure me to consent. I feel like I should be by their side to protect them. I look again at Dana whose eyes have not budged from the TV screen. After a moment of silence, she peers over at me. Her glare tells me she's confused as to why I'm not answering.

"Sure, I'll follow you guys," I finally say.

Dana's eyes spit rage, but she surrenders. "Fine. I'll go too."

13

THE CONVENTION

Here we are at the student convention. Today's plan is for all students to observe and ask questions pertaining to different areas of work-related fields. But who cares about that when the world is going to end in four years? Four years means that I won't have a real career. I won't have all the things I once wanted. The future I envisioned for myself is gone. Four years isn't time enough to finish my education. So why would I waste my time in school, stuck in books and lessons, when everything *important* is about to become so *insignificant*. My future is no longer what I wanted it to be. I've been destined to save humanity, to bring the surviving humans to a distant planet.

And yet, I have to play along anyhow. It seems fun to play pretend for a day – pretend I'll be something later other than the saviour of the world. I don't think the convention has *that* job description listed.

The students are still descending from the buses. With the crowd getting larger, I can hardly find Dana and the others. But then I hear someone call me. The source came from somewhere by the left wall. The structure in this downtown area isn't very large, but it's really tall. It's old architecture: red brick, arched doorways outlined with white blocks. I was told a great fire had consumed a good part of the city some ten years ago. That's why this section of the city looks more modern in its structures. And it also explains why only the top half of the convention center is built with glass windows all around.

The voice calls me again. I push through the crowd and find Scotty, Seleste, Brydhen, Dana, and another girl I suspect to be Sandra, all huddled together by the wall. Dana is attached to Brydhen's left arm, holding on romantically, her eyes shimmering with happiness. That's not new. Brydhen and Dana have been acting personal for a while now. Every time they've been spotted together, they're close to each other. Lovingly. It hurts a lot to see them that way. It's like my worst nightmare unfolding before my eyes. Why? Because of something I'm afraid to say out loud, or even admit to myself: I think I have feelings for Brydhen too.

Scotty is completely ignoring them, something I should be doing as well. It doesn't seem to bother Richard. He's the only one who's been nice to me. Attentive to my feelings. But he's not here today. The person who's never usually there is Sandra. For someone who is so interested in activities, she doesn't seem as enthusiastic to take part in them. While I'm thinking about it, I haven't seen her very often at school either. Her absences are very strange. But I hear she's always sick and has recurrent asthma attacks.

As she stands before me right now, I notice she's smaller than me, and wears discoloured jeans and a thick, blue cotton sweater. Sandra has such deep brown eyes they almost look black. Her face is round, like the rest of her. Other than that, I know nothing about her. Note to self: learn more about Sandra.

The crowd of students finally starts pushing through the doors and inside the building. According to what Scotty tells me, our school is approximately ten minutes south from where we are. It makes this a prime location and this event a perfect target.

I follow behind Dana and Brydhen. Just looking at them clenches my heart. And when Dana looks over her shoulder to make sure I'm there, I force myself to fake a smile. Truthfully, I just want to cry and die inside.

"Are you feeling okay?" Seleste asks me.

I answer with a smile. The honest answer is 'no,' but I don't want to attract attention. I don't want people to know how I feel. It's wrong to feel this way, especially when my best friend is happy.

"Are you ready to get attacked by monstrous aliens?" Brydhen says, with a bit too much excitement. It's a little masochistic to be excited by the prospect of getting attacked.

"Sure," Dana responds, annoyingly passive-aggressive.

"It'll be fun!" Scotty exclaims. "We'll have front row seats to the action."

"You guys are crazy," I respond. There's no way they could have already forgotten the incident at the theatre. Not long ago, they were almost killed.

As soon as we cross the threshold of the convention center, I lose track of everyone. They go in different directions from the lobby. The latter leads off in three wings: North for all business, marketing, computer programming, military, government positions, and any other worldwide field; South wing for medical and science jobs, education, schooling, university positions, all other humanities fields; and East wing for any other service fields.

Most people go in the East wing, including Scotty.

Seleste and Dana go together in the South wing, and Brydhen in the North. I don't see where Sandra goes. And as I watch them all leave me in the lobby, I ponder my next move.

Do I stay in the lobby and wait for trouble? Do I continue pretending that I'm a normal human being with a desire to work in one specific field for the rest of my life?

Every bone in my body rejects the idea, but my brain is telling me otherwise. I should try to live like the others.

I eventually come to a decision. I head toward the south wing. If I'm going to be anything other than a superhero, I'll be a veterinarian. I've always loved animals. It's only natural I should help treat them. That's something I can see myself doing for the rest of my life. Unfortunately, that's only a fantasy. You'd think fantasy would be the superhero part of my life. But it's the other way around. It's what I've come to understand as a normal way of life that is so unreal now.

I head down the carpeted hall. There are no windows, just white lights all along the hallway, each one of them opening onto large presentation rooms. Projectors are set up, chairs placed in rows, and few people sitting or standing in each room. It feels so formal and official that I'm beginning to stress about the concept of sitting in a room with random people and listening to an adult who thinks he or she knows it all.

I'm just being judgemental. I know. It must be the stress.

I find the room marked *Vet, Animal Rescue*. The white paper is taped on the door and indicates the time slot allocated to the conference. It reads, *Lecture, 10:30 AM – 12:30 PM*. I look at my watch and sigh in despair. It's only 8:45 AM. I have a long time to wait. That explains why the room is empty.

I look up and down the hall. I find the exit sign to my right. The door at the end of the hallway is for emergency exits only. It likely leads straight onto the street. To my left, about a dozen doors away, is the lobby. I can't tell if the structure of the building allows for safe exit in the case of an attack. If creatures find a way to block all ends of the building, everyone is trapped inside. But if they don't, then there's a multitude of possible exits.

I look again to the emergency exit. The door seems to be covered by a metal plate, reflecting the light from the overhead. But as I observe it, it becomes clearer. At first it looks like someone is at the end of the hall. The skin colour is the same shade of grey as the uniform walls. But as my eyes analyze the humanoid form, I realize it's not human at all. In fact, it looks like a demon: a combination of two horse legs, a bear torso wearing a protective silver chest plate, arms of a gorilla allowing it to maneuver a large, spiked club for a weapon, and the head of something I've never seen before. The head looks reptilian, but slimy, the eyes yellow on the side of its head, not in the front.

For a moment, I stare at it, puzzled by its presence and intentions. It's not moving. It's just guarding the end of the hall.

It's guarding the emergency exit.

I let myself be distracted by someone calling my name. The moment I look back is the moment the creature disappears. Did it go up the stairs? No. I would see the door closing behind it. The same is true for the exit. So where did it go? How could it have vanished just like that? How did it even appear there without me noticing? Or am I going crazy and seeing things?

I look again toward the lobby. It's Sandra. She called my name perfectly on time with the creature's disappearance. As I walk to her, the overhead light casts strange shadows on her face. Her dark hair hangs in front of her face. Creepy.

"We're all in the lobby," she says. Her voice is strange too. Rough. Sickly. It sounds like a bad cold.

"Oh," I respond. Everyone else must have conferences beginning later too.

"They're going to the cafeteria. Get some breakfast," she informs me.

I wonder if she's always spoken this way. Sentences cut short. Threatening-like. I'm not sure if she wants me to get breakfast, or if the others are getting food. She's very confusing to me already, and this is my first conversation with her.

"I'll tag along," I decide to say. "And you?"

"I'm not hungry," she answers.

The shadows on her face move. Or flinch. They almost look alive, like they're not caused by the overhead lights. But that's impossible.

"Me neither, but I'm going," I tell her.

"I'm not," she says coolly. "I'll stay here."

"Okay. Suit yourself."

I walk past her. Her eyes follow me until I'm out of sight, but she doesn't turn or follow. Sandra just stands there, watching the hallway. Maybe she saw the monster too. Is she keeping an eye on it? Could she be Dragoon? If so, her voice is quite different. Her appearance too. Perhaps that's a perk to the transformation. I should notice next time I transform if my voice changes too.

But… Sandra as Dragoon?

Sandra as super-human?

Sandra is creepy and unsettling. Dragoon is the complete opposite.

I see Dana wave in the air, attracting my attention. I walk to her and the others. I'm relieved to find that Dana and Brydhen have finally learned the meaning of personal space.

A scream rips the air: a horrible high-pitch scream – a cry for help. The voices in the lobby drop to a few whispers. People move discreetly. Others run to aid. Some try to push through a crowd to get a closer look at the incident.

The lobby doors shut. More screams. My ears track them quickly. As suspected, the screams originate from each hallway.

That means all exits have been blocked.

That means everyone is trapped inside.

We're all quarantined in the lobby.

I look at Brydhen and Scotty. This is what they wanted. They should really be careful what they wish for. They look worried now, like they no longer want this to happen. Despite this, they have their camera phones ready to record the event.

How do you want Kitsune to protect you when she can't transform? At least, not in front of all these people.

14

RIVALRY

I contemplate the room. Three hallways blocked by strange-looking monsters. People are shuffling in all directions, trying to find a way out, pushing each other, shoving one another. Strange how the human race will stop at nothing to survive - even if it means putting others' lives in danger.

Some people trip over their feet, others fall and get hurt, while some are getting angry. A group of teachers rallied at the front entrance are trying to figure out a way to pry the doors open. They try to pull as a group, set the doors on fire, and finally, when all else fails, bang on the door and yell for help.

This is all too familiar. The doors magically blocked, a group of students at the mercy of whatever danger will appear, and me, trying to find a safe place to transform.

"Kass!" a voice calls behind me. I turn to find Brydhen reaching out to me. He grabs my arms in panic and utters, "Dana's gone!"

The word 'gone' immediately translates as 'dead' in my mind. But I knew it couldn't be true. Dana was safe as long as she stayed in the middle of the crowd.

"What do you mean she's gone?" I ask Brydhen. His eyes express pain and worry. "What happened?"

"I don't know," he yells over the din of people screaming. "One second we're watching the profs at the entrance and the other Dana runs in the crowd and disappears."

"Why didn't you go after her?" I retort with distinct blame in my voice.

"I'm sorry," he musters.

"Never mind," I tell him. "I'll go get her. Which way did she go?"

"That way I think," Brydhen tells me while pointing to the left hallway.

Stupid Dana. Didn't she learn from the first time at the theatre? What was she thinking running toward the screams? Any sensible person would run the other way.

I run in the direction Brydhen thought she went. I have to push my way past students running against me. I can see the monsters slowly advancing toward the lobby. They're checking every room along the hall - probably to make sure they got everyone. But what did they do with the students when they found them hiding in a room? Let them go? Or kill them?

At the theatre, the creatures would not have hesitated to murder, or eat, students. I honestly don't think it's any different now. Would Dana have gone by herself in a room to hide? Would she have left all of us behind for her own survival? It just doesn't seem like her. I don't think she would do that. So why did she leave the group?

I push a door open to my left and find three adolescents cowering in the far-right corner of the room. The girl's face is hidden away in her hands, but I can see her tears trickling down her arms. The boy to her left has an arm around her shoulders. His legs are shaking. The boy to her right is calm and expressionless. I observe them for a moment until the sound of chattered glass has me yelling for them to get out and go to the lobby where they would be safer than here.

They reluctantly stand. I urge them to hurry, or they could die. They cross the threshold, their faces white and blank. Finally alone in the room, I transform into Kitsune. I should have known this event wouldn't go by without her. I'd bet anything Dragoon is here too.

I escape the room quickly. The monsters are two doors away from me. They spot me and pause. I slowly back up toward the lobby. This makes one of them growl at me and blow smoke from its nose.

I freeze.

Now I hear the sirens approaching. Police. Ambulance. Firefighters. The deluxe. I turn quickly and run to the lobby, provoking the monsters to follow me. When reaching the crowd, I look over my shoulder and see them where I was standing before. But they don't go any further. I'd almost go as far as to say that they won't, or can't, come closer. It's like they're only there to scare everyone and kill those who stray from the group.

I notice the crowd moving into a circle. I look up. The glass window ten levels up is shattered. I push through to the center of their circle.

What I find is horrifying.

The three students I forced out of the classroom and many others are lying on the floor, glass shards protruding from their innocent bodies. There's a pool of blood forming beneath them.

It's ugly to look at.

And it's all my fault.

I told them to come here. I told them they would be safe. I forced them to their deaths.

I should have protected them. I should have been here.

My eyes are wet with tears, but I don't let them fall. My heart is heavy with guilt … up until I see her. Dragoon. She's among the students lying on the floor.

Except she's not hurt.

She's *not* dead.

She's the one who must have broken the glass, causing half a dozen students to die.

My blood boils and I feel my face go hot with rage.

It's *not* my fault.

They would have been safe if it wasn't for *her*!

I march over to her, carefully stepping over people – dead people – soaking my boots in blood, staining red the bottom of my uniform. I furiously clutch Dragoon's throat to lift her up, forcing her to regain consciousness.

She looks into my face.

At first, she looks puzzled, aware of my grip on her skin. She peers around us at the crowd, analyzing their faces and their reactions.

Then she sees it.

The blood.

The bodies.

I release her neck and let her absorb what she's done. I see her chest pump faster, her breathing quickening, her mouth slightly open.

She's in shock.

I suddenly feel bad for her. She must have been attacked trying to defend innocent people, and instead was propelled through a window ten stories above us.

Dragoon didn't mean for this to happen.

But it did.

And I can't help but be furious with her.

The landing of something heavy behind me suddenly breaks the silence. By the shuffling of people's feet as they scurry away and their screams of panic, I know something bad is going to happen next.

I don't have time to look behind me, but I can feel the presence of something very large. Something warm and hairy captures my neck, and instantly, I hear a loud *crack*. A shock vibrates my body, and my head feels on fire. I realize my view is cricked. My body falls limp, gravity claiming my weight. Lying there, I can feel the warmth of the blood on the carpeted floor saturating my skin.

But why am I still conscious, unable to blink, unable to move, but still cognitively aware?

And then it comes to me: my neck is broken. All the sounds are confused, blended together in one harmonious orchestra of screams and gasps.

I'm more disoriented than worried for my well-being. Everyone probably thinks I'm dead. I should be. But clearly, I'm not. Or is this what it feels like to slowly lose all life? Will my vision fail, then will I lose oxygen, then will I fade away? Or is my super body resisting death? Even though I'm not really in a position to choose my fate, I convince myself it's the latter.

I wait for any response from my body. But none comes. Not instantly.

I lie here helpless, feeling really stupid.

Dragoon shoots off the ground, splattering my visage with red-hot liquid. Urgency finally sinks in and I'm afraid I won't be able to come back from this. My main fear is that my body won't recover this time.

I don't know what happened last time I almost died. According to all sources, all lights went out and then my body disappeared from the scene. No one was able to see my body revert back to its human identity, if indeed the transformation cancels out when I die, or when my energy drains quickly. I don't want to find out today if I revert back because my body is faced with death. Everyone will know that Kitsune is in fact Kassidy.

My thoughts are fuzzy. I should be worried about dying, not the fate of my identity. But I don't feel like I'm dying. I feel, and I truly want to believe, that my body is resilient to muscle damage and broken bones that would ultimately lead to death for a regular person. My body doesn't work like others'.

Like a sharp knife in my throat, something locks back into place, shooting a bright light in my skull. For a moment, I'm completely blind, but the instantaneous pain significantly surpasses all other details of my recovery.

I scream loudly, my body shaking from the stress.

I sit up, feeling sick from the sight of my body drenched in teenage blood. My body purges my breakfast in flakes of beige and orange. The acid burns my throat, adding to the muscle pain I already feel. It's like a bad hangover, and the result of hours of bad sleep.

I try to get passed the disorientation and the discomfort. I immediately search my face for the sign of a mask. It's there. I hadn't reverted back to my human form.

I force myself on my feet and manage to scamper toward the exit – the locked doors holding everyone hostage in the building. From what I can tell, the monsters didn't do any physical damage to anyone else other than Dragoon and myself. The death of those teenagers was the fault of no one directly. But before things get worse, I need to open those doors and let everyone out.

I don't understand why quarantining students in this building is any use if they're not the prime targets. Was the witch setting a trap to draw Dragoon and I out? Were *we* the targets, and the students the bait?

As I reach the doors, I feel the stares of everyone around. They can't believe I'm still standing. *I* can hardly believe it myself. But my super body is regaining the energy it had a few minutes ago. I can feel the surge of power run through my veins and the rush of adrenaline pushing my body forward.

I take hold of the metal bars on the doors and try to pull them. Dizziness overwhelms me for a moment, but I try again. The bright spots in my vision blind me momentarily.

I tighten my grip on the metal bars, feeling my pulse at the tip of my fingers. I give precise pulls with the same amount of strength, at exactly the same intervals. I silently encourage myself, willing the doors to open miraculously. I'm still trying to adapt to the blinding flashes in my vision when I exhibit force on the doors. But I refuse to give up. I refuse to let these people worry for their lives any longer.

In four years from now, most, or all of these people will die from disease or infection. It's my job, my destiny to make sure they survive for as long as possible.

A boy, most probably my age, reaches around me, takes hold of the metal bar. He pulls at the same time as me, the difficulty of the task appearing in his frown. At first, there's just him, but then a few others come to help. We receive praise and encouragement from the crowd behind.

When the mystical seal on the doors finally breaks, the fresh city air is welcomed in the lobby. The scent of death is overwhelming, and the crowd is unmistakably anxious to escape the constraints of the building. I move out of the way and let the people rush out onto the street. I'm patted on the shoulder, thanked, and complimented on my bravery and honour. I feel so important to their eyes – if only they knew what their future holds.

The severity of the situation comes back to me. I rush to the center of the lobby where I try to ignore the bodies on the floor to my right. This reminds me of the dry sticky liquid itching my skin and staining my uniform. I feel the necessity to cleanse my body, but I know that washing away the blood will not take away the guilt or remorse weighing heavy on my heart.

I concentrate on Dragoon's aura. I can feel her power, like waves emanating, reaching out to me …

From the sixteenth floor!

I push off the floor and break through the glass window.

Dragoon's aura is fading quickly. I speed in her direction. I find her on all fours, gasping for breath, battered, and horribly bruised.

A group of monsters heads toward her, stomping threateningly with all their might. Their clubs are raised, ready to swoosh down for another blow, most likely destined for Dragoon's head.

I run to her, lift her against me, and jump back into the hall just in time. The club misses me by inches. We collide against a brick wall, tearing it down as we land together. I hear Dragoon's faint voice whisper to me.

"You're alive."

"Yeah, get over it," I tell her, feeling the hurry to escape the monsters headed straight for us, although there's no rush in their footing.

"Why are you helping me?" Dragoon whimpers.

"What happened?" I ask her, ignoring her question. I collect myself and rush to my feet. I once again force Dragoon against me and carry her along the hall.

"They attacked me from behind. They must have darted me with something." She breathed heavily, her chest struggling with the oxygen pumping her lungs. "Because they've been beating me down ever since …"

I know she means the teenagers in the lobby. I test her theory and set Dragoon down against a wall some way down the hallway to inspect her body. At first, I see only blood and ripped clothes. Then a minuscule white thorn captures my attention. It's hardly noticeable on Dragoon's spine, but I pull it out and examine it closely. It looks like simple debris that could have fallen from the walls or picked up on the floor. But the power in my eyes allows me to see the markings around the flat surface of the top. It's not something I recognize, so I make a mental note to show it to Alcidor – if ever we see him again. I thrust the thorn in the pocket on my thigh.

"Why are you helping me?" Dragoon repeats. This time she coughs out blood. She wipes the string of saliva and chunks of red-wine blood hanging from her bottom lip.

Again, I ignore her question. The monsters are in the hallway, staring at us. But they don't move. To me, they feel more threatening by their immobility than by intending an attack on us.

Dragoon tries to stand on her own, but gravity forces her back to the floor. "Get us out of here," she whispers, her head hunched over as though she's falling asleep.

And I do.

I reach around Dragoon's waist, snatch her up into my arms, and just as the monsters realize we're planning an escape and run thunderously to us, I break through the glass and through the opposite wall. Once outside into the sunlight, I hear Dragoon's very low voice whisper over to me.

"They won't follow, will they?"

I wonder the same thing. But I can't be sure. There's no way to know. If they exit the building, we'll be responsible for anyone else who gets hurt. And now, what will Brydhen and the gang think of Kitsune and Dragoon? Will they believe we're not the bad guys? Will they believe we're here to save them – or as many of them as possible?

So, I land on the roof of the adjacent building. I need to keep an eye on the convention center in case anything *leaks* out. Dragoon squirms in my arms in order to also look at the building. Her movements against my body remind me that I'm wounded and in pain. My muscles are tense and cramped. I wish I could let her go, but I know that if I do, she will fall, and probably won't be able to get back up.

Just as it feels like it's been forever that we've been waiting for something to happen, I see the paramedics and a few men in blue jumpsuits carry out occupied black body bags. I shake on the inside and feel so guilty at the loss of those who lost their lives today. They were so innocent and fragile. A scary thought occurs to me: these deaths are only the beginning.

My arms are suddenly relieved of Dragoon's weight. They are numb with exhaustion. Dragoon has completely vanished. She didn't fly away, or teleport. She just disappeared. I guess that's what happened to us when we fought the spider and Predzellmoo. I want to think that she's with Alcidor, recovering from her wounds. Who knows where she is? As long as she's safe.

Alcidor told us to work together, and even if I'm still angry with Dragoon for the death of innocents, I still have to work with her no matter what. I know their deaths were no one's fault. A great part of me blames Dragoon, and another part of me blames myself. But I know I can't save everyone. My sanity will not survive feeling responsible for all the lives that will be lost over the course of the upcoming four years.

DANA

15

HALLOWEEN

I was prepared to die.

At least, I think I was. But Kitsune saved me at the student convention. I knew it was her because of her aura, her strength. I don't know if it's creepy or ingenious – to be this connected to her.

It's because of that connection that I knew she wasn't gone when the monster broke her neck. I could still feel her, her heartbeat. I had to get out of there, so the monster would follow me and everyone else would be safe. But everything else after that is a blur. I can't recall at which point I was stung by something pointy, and then I couldn't stand on my own two feet. And Kitsune was there for me. Again.

I juggle my memory for any other detail, but nothing comes to mind.

I look out the kitchen window as I silently eat dinner with my family. The sky is getting darker. It doesn't look like it's going to be a good Halloween night. Cole is in such a hurry. There's nothing else on his mind but the candy he's going to collect tonight. My sister is just as grumpy as ever because of yet another argument she had with my mom. I don't know about what, and honestly, I couldn't care less. I've got things on my mind too.

To start, an alien is responsible for my powers.

An *alien*.

Just that fact in itself is so unbelievable. And it's not like I can tell my parents about any of it. I mean, where would I even start? Hey, mom, dad, an alien named Alcidor altered my DNA without my consent, gave me powers, and enlisted me to save as many humans as possible against a race of alien witches. Oh, and by the way, the world is coming to an end in four years from now.

I can't say that to them.

And I certainly can't face the ensuing questions. I'd hate for them to ask me if they'll be alive in four years' time, if I'll be able to protect them, or if because they're my family, they'll get a special place in the rescue rocket ship off this rock.

I have zero answers for those questions.

I try to make sense of all that information. It doesn't seem like much, but the weight of it keeps me up at night. I can't seem to close my eyes long enough to get any rest at all. My heart beats hard in my ears and I sweat profusely every night, every time I try to close my eyes. I can't help but imagine the worst scenarios possible. Maybe water will run out long before

Alcidor expects it to, or maybe people are going to go crazy, and one idiot somewhere is going to launch missiles and atomic bombs.

I'm terrified. I'm trembling all the time.

I can't cope. Everyday could be my last, but I have to live like it's just another typical day. I mean, where's the sense in that? There are monsters out there, there's been attacks, innocent people dying. And yet, it's Halloween anyway? Let's just send our children out in the streets to collect candy like none of this is actually happening. Let's close our eyes to the horrors of reality.

It drives me crazy.

I don't think I have much of a choice, though. My little brother's going to be out there tonight, and so will Kassidy. For some reason, she's also tempted by the prospect of free candy.

Watch me be so *impressed* right now.

But I have to be honest with myself. I'd rather be out there to keep an eye out. What else am I going to do? Stay inside and pout?

Hell no.

Cole and I slowly make our way to Kassidy's home a block away, observing the black clouds rolling above us.

"Thunderstorm?" he asks behind his Scream mask.

The gust of wind becomes angrier, the tops of the trees lean west, and their leaves blow away in the street.

"Yup," I answer. "We'll do as many houses as we can before it gets too bad."

"We better," Cole replies, a bit of a threat lingering in his words.

Kassidy opens the door and welcomes us inside her home just long enough to grab her bag and her umbrella. Good idea. I didn't think of bringing an umbrella. It would have been a smart thing to do, but my thoughts are all over the place to concentrate on anything else.

The rumble in the sky is threatening. But it doesn't discourage Kassidy and Cole. Their addiction for candy drives them to keep going from door to door. Most people aren't surprised to see my brother, but they're taken off guard when Kass presents her pillowcase too. She may be dressed as a brown belt, aikido fighter, but she's practically an adult.

We only have the time to walk a few streets when the weather worsens. Now the rain is coming down like sharp knives and the wind is blowing away everything on the street. Kassidy pulls out her umbrella quickly, but it turns inside out from the strength of the wind. She curses, and Cole and I laugh.

"I think you need a new -" he begins, but an explosion behind us cuts his sentence short.

We fly forward and roll to a stop on the hard, wet ground.

"What was that?" I ask angrily, hoping Kassidy hears me over the growling of the thunder. I hold my head in bewilderment.

Cole is about a meter away, in complete alarm. He takes off his mask and I can see the blood dripping from his temple.

"Cole!" I shout and reach out to him.

I rip a part of his sleeve and hold it to his temple. Cole immediately starts to cry.

Now I'm angry.

Kassidy answers, "I don't know." She slowly brings herself to sit on the slippery ground. She whispers something else under her breath, but I can't quite make out her words. I overlook it on the account that my brother is hurt and crying.

But a feeling sends a shiver down my spine.

There's something in the ground, right below our feet, and it's chosen this specific time and place to come out.

I look over at the source of the explosion, and it dawns on me.

I watch Predzellmoo maneuver its slimy form onto the pavement. But I don't understand why it's here. My friends are under the impression every attack is student-related. But we're far from school. So, is this attack random? Or did the witch discovered me, and she knows where I live?

I bring myself to my feet immediately and quickly help Cole up. I force him to run with me over to Kassidy. She is poised to the spot, her eyes fixed on the material slithering our way. The brown muck I remember from our previous battle looks black under the rain. There's no obstacle for the creature; no rocks or rubble or water puddle stops the *thing* from expanding into a wide circle. Whatever it's made of, it envelops everything. I reach Kassidy just in time to pull her back a meter.

Predzellmoo ceases to expand, and, from the middle of the brown mud-like material, it begins to take form. It sucks in all the substance it initially spread out, shaping arms and curves. We can make out the torso from the skirt that starts to form at the bottom. I see two dark pits forming near the top, what I fear will become the sockets to its eyes.

"I think right now is our cue to run," I say in Kassidy's ear, while holding Cole close to my chest. I hadn't realized that we had sunk onto the pavement.

I sit there, clenching Cole close to me. A part of me doesn't want this to be real. But another part of me is speaking another language altogether. It's like a rush of running water against your skin; a cold chill running up your spine; utmost fright sending shivers along your entire body. The adrenaline pulses through me. It pounds hard and true in my blood.

"Cole," I say over the din of the thunder and rain and pushing him to his feet. "Run home, don't look back. I'll be right behind you." But Cole doesn't move. He watches Predzellmoo take form, and I know too well what happens next.

"Cole!" I yell to bring him back to me. This time I push him. He hesitates, but then he runs out of sight.

I shake my head. Rebellious thoughts rage in my mind faster than I can find the courage to stand on my feet again. But Kassidy is anxious to stand, and this forces me to do the same. I clutch her sleeve, and we instinctively decide to run together, following the very few people left on the street.

I presume this is the part where I'm supposed to find an excuse to separate from Kassidy, find a nice dark place to transform, but I run like death is chasing me. Kassidy follows me. She has a harder time than I do, and I forget that I'm driven by superhero power while she's not. I slow down for her.

"Wait," Kassidy whispers and comes to a stop, her hot breath emitting smoke from her mouth.

"What?" I ask her.

I let her breathe for a moment. The rain is softer now. And although most of the clouds have blown away, the sky is still painted navy blue. There is no moon tonight to give us light – only the lampposts stationed every half a dozen houses. I blink on my night vision right away. I can see Predzellmoo has not moved. He's still observing his surroundings. Obviously, he's confused.

"I just needed to breathe! Is it following us?" Kassidy asks me, looking over her shoulder.

"No," I answer, also looking over her shoulder.

An explosion shakes the ground, scaring the life right out of me. My first reflex is to duck and cover my head. But it's no use. The house is a block away, where we left Predzellmoo.

What I fear the most goes up in flame in front of me. We can see the fire rising above the other roofs. That could have been my house, and my family. Were there children in that house? Parents? Puppies?

"Let's get out of here," Kassidy murmurs.

Her eyes are fixed on the site of the blazing pyre. She's just as traumatized as I am. The only words resounding through my mind are, *oh my god*. There's a deepening feeling of helplessness building in me – a realization that I have no control over anything that may happen. Even with these powers, I can't save everyone.

I'm just here to make sure *some* people survive.

Kassidy turns back to me. Her eyes are glowing with tears. She won't look at me straight in the face. "Let's go," she breathes.

I agree. At the next crossroads, we separate. I walk in my driveway while she continues forward. She speeds up her pace as soon as our hands release one another. We'd been holding on so tightly after the explosion, I almost forgot the feeling of blood in my fingers.

I rush to the back of my house where I transform immediately.

There's nothing else in my heart but cold vengeance.

16

GLACIER COLD

It just stands there, immobile, and unnerved. It's watching the flames dance from the shattered windows, the snakes of fire licking the walls and eating away at everything in its path. I land right by the creature with such force I cause a crater the size of my bedroom. But Predzellmoo takes no notice of me. The burning fire has caught its attention; it's completely mesmerized.

"You won't get away with this," I say loudly.

Predzellmoo ignores me again.

"What is he doing?" I hear Kitsune's voice behind me.

I don't look at her, but Predzellmoo does. His head jerks in her direction suddenly. Kitsune's voice brought him out of a reverie and his eyes are now locked on her.

Again, I hear Kitsune ask, "What is he doing?" This time her high pitch tone is vibrant with concern.

I still don't answer Kitsune. Honestly, I don't know what Predzellmoo is doing, or what it's intending to do next. But all I care about are the people it murdered. That creature bombed those homes like it was nothing – and now nothing will stop me from avenging those who lost their lives. They were innocent!

The images of the teenagers who died on *my* account at the convention center flash before my eyes. The blood, the smell, and the guilt come rushing back to me. It's like stepping out into a snowstorm right after a shower, when your hair is still wet. It freezes instantly, becomes icicles; your vision is blurred by the wind blowing into your teary eyes; and the dry, winter cold travels to your bones instantly. Your heart feels like it's going to stop beating and you gasp for breath. But eventually, you adapt. Eventually, you find a safe and warm place to settle.

Right now, there's nothing but the cold wind and the sensation of unforgivable remorse and shame in my heart. All these attacks, and all these deaths are on my hands.

And Predzellmoo's.

That monster will pay for everyone who died. Especially after all it's done. Since its first apparition, Predzellmoo's blown up buildings, houses, cars, and helicopters. It's killed more people than I can count with my fingers. And since it has no other purpose in life but to destroy everything and anything, then I'm going to take its life.

"Why is he coming toward me like that?" Kitsune asks me, her voice just as high.

Predzellmoo's body is swerving from side to side, slowly progressing toward Kitsune. For a clearer picture, it's like a zombie carefully approaching a new prey: it's horrifying.

I stay silent, attentive to each of the creature's movements, watching for any ticks or signs of an impending attack. It's now a meter from me, and it's like I'm not even here.

Predzellmoo's focus is Kitsune. And perhaps she is its life-long ambition. Just like a peasant to an unattainable goddess, precious and fragile, it can't approach faster or more carefully. It's like it's afraid that she will, like a fox, scuttle away and disappear forever.

At this point, the streets are empty of people. They've all gone to seek shelter. The rain has ended, the clouds have gone, but the darkness has stayed behind. Only my night vision guides me now.

I hear a shuffle behind me, and by Predzellmoo's immobilization, I know Kitsune has backed away.

"*Fox girl*," it says.

"It's looking for you," I immediately tell Kitsune. I'm careful to speak slowly and softly, so not to invite an attack. Any sudden movements can change the rules of the game.

But what game are we playing? The answer is right in front of us: it's Predzellmoo's game. It's a creature with a fascination for Kitsune, and an inconsolable desire to get close to her. Even if we're not in control of the monster's next move, we can still take advantage of this situation.

"No, he's not," Kitsune responds. Her voice is rough, like she didn't like my comment. But it makes Predzellmoo's body jerk slightly forward as though Kitsune was about to bounce away any second and it wanted to catch her in the palm of its muddy hand.

"Predzellmoo love fox girl," it announces. Its voice sounds like someone trying to talk with their mouth full of toothpaste and water - an unappealing gurgling sound that makes you want to gag.

"Fox girl not love Predzellmoo," Kitsune responds ever so softly. She has her palms up in front of her now, like she's expecting an attack and she wants to show it that she's harmless.

"Predzellmoo hurt," it replies.

The monster's voice is annoying now. I just want to shut it up. Kill it, if possible. The guilt and the anger inside me still bite at my core. The ice crackles on my bones while a chilling silence resonates within me.

"Help me?" Kitsune implores, more as a suggestion.

"No," I say flatly, trying wildly to hold back a snort. Unless she means to kill it, like right now. And that would be the end of it. It's a monster. It's a danger to us all.

"Predzellmoo love fox girl," it repeats, louder. The gurgling sounds are muddier this time, like it needs us to be attentive.

"Fox girl NOT LOVE Predzellmoo," Kitsune yells back. She takes another cautious step backward, careful not to spark a negative response from the creature.

"I don't think it cares about your feelings. It's declaring its love to *you*," I inform her, like it wasn't obvious enough.

Predzellmoo still doesn't seem to respond to the sound of my voice, so I continue. "How about you take care of that thing once and for all, and this time, don't let it get away."

Kitsune turns to me. The folds around the edges of her mask tell me she's at least upset with me, maybe angry. I can't really tell for sure. But to be completely honest, I don't really care either. The creature can't get out of this alive again. And I'm not interested in Kitsune's feelings toward me.

Her stare is incessant. And it's like her entire body is flaring with energy. It looks like ocean waves roaring out of her.

The ground shakes – equal vibrations, almost like they're following the tempo of a metronome.

The tremors become increasingly violent now. I have to readjust my legs to keep my balance. The street shatters. Blocks of asphalt break apart and fall deep within the fissures.

Then suddenly, water gushes out from below and showers us. All three of us are immobile, watching the wave roar from the crack in the street. It keeps coming and doesn't stop. Drenched all over again, I realize we're standing in the portion of the street that's concave compared to the rest of the area. It's essentially the one spot that keeps all the rain and forces it down the storm drain. But the drain must have collapsed because the water level in the street is rising quickly. Within moments, I have water up to my knees. Here and in the crater I caused earlier, water rushes higher and higher.

The trembling of the street ceases but the shower of water keeps coming. I peer over at Kitsune. She doesn't appear impacted by the earth quakes, or bothered by the water.

Then it comes to me. Like a bright light turning on above a cartoon character's head, the realization of Kitsune's powers dawns on me.

"You're doing this," I murmur, completely baffled by what I'm witnessing.

Kitsune smirks.

I almost forget about Predzellmoo up to this point. I'm so distracted by all the action I forget the most dangerous threat still in the vicinity. I can't read any expression in its mud-like visage, but I can tell that the water isn't suiting its body. It's slowly losing form, its body liquefying within seconds. The brown guck that I currently see as dark green due to my night vision is spreading out.

"Me love fox girl," Predzellmoo says, still as determined to reach the fox that could sprint away at any moment.

"Fox don't like *you*!" Kitsune exclaims.

She raises her palms to the sky, and like out of a special effects movie, two large strings of water rise like snakes. And as Kitsune's palms rush out toward Predzellmoo, so do the water snakes.

The rush of water pouring from above overwhelms Predzellmoo. The creature is thrust back into the basin by two rushing columns of water.

"Not so tough after all," I hear Kitsune mutter to herself.

But she's wrong.

She thinks she got him, but I know better. I see the shadow beneath the water, the large entity manipulating its material embodiment to move forward like a shark. Kitsune looks proud of herself, but she doesn't realize that Predzellmoo moves around her legs and is slowly molding again behind her. The body towers over her. The deep sockets in its head for the great white eyes form.

"You're so caught up in your awesomeness that you forgot to follow-up on your attack," I say, resisting the urge to insult Kitsune.

I imitate Kitsune's gestures, but instead of raising my palms to the sky, I lift one straight in front of me. I feel my palm go hot, but it's a degree I can handle. It's not painful, nor is it painless. It's more of an agreeable tickle in the heart of my hand. There, I see a fireball instantaneously materializing.

17

DROWNING

I will the fireball forward. Launching from my hand with great speed, it leaves behind only a shimmer. It's like a string of light outlining its trajectory from my hand to its target. It glows with a beautiful and bright red and blue. In a split second, it rushes past Kitsune's ear.

Bull's eye.

"What are you doing?" Kitsune yells at me. She sounds taken aback, maybe even angry with me. "It's not me you're supposed to attack!"

Kitsune must think I was aiming for her, and that I just missed because it's my first time using this power. I really want to dismiss her right now, but I just can't help but retort back. "It wasn't you I attacked either."

My answer is no comfort to her. By her reply, I know she didn't listen to my words. "You could have killed me, or badly injure me! What were you thinking? I'm not the enemy here."

"I'm trying to protect you!"

Now I'm really frustrated. Her melodrama and exaggeration are too much.

I shouldn't have helped her. Kitsune should deal with her own problems. After all, Predzellmoo isn't interested in me. But it was, however, seeking refuge behind Kitsune. Maybe it thought I wouldn't attack if it was standing so close behind her.

Although it was utterly wrong, I have to admit I'm a little impressed with the monster's ability to strategize.

"Yeah right," Kitsune retorts in disbelief. She makes me feel like I'm a liar and making up excuses to hurt her. Now I wish that were true. "And what *were* you attacking, then?"

Frowning from the anger I feel, I cock my head to the side and point behind her. Kitsune wheels around easily in the water. And now she sees it. Predzellmoo is splattered against the front wall of a brick house. There are pieces of guck on the surface of the water forming a trail from where Predzellmoo was to where it is now.

I wait for Kitsune to apologize, but she doesn't move, and she doesn't say anything. Instead, we both watch as Predzellmoo's pieces of guck slowly regroup. But it's not taking form again. Instead of materializing above water, the mud-like material reorganizes as a giant puddle like oil under water. Its movements are agile and swift. Seconds later, Predzellmoo surfaces again only metres from me, dead centre between Kitsune and I.

I ready for an attack.

Predzellmoo hurls its arm straight at me. I know it intends another explosion, but my body and reflexes are quicker. Before the thought has completely crossed my mind, I'm already in mid-dive sideways.

And something unpredictable happens.

Predzellmoo must have foreseen my reaction, or it's beginning to understand our battle instincts better than ourselves. Its arm is headed right for me, and if it reaches me, I know I'm a goner.

Just as I submerge, I hear Kitsune scream, "NO."

I stay beneath the water, expecting for Predzellmoo's hand to attain me. But nothing comes. I bring myself to my feet and inspect the field.

Kitsune's left palm is pointing at nowhere in particular, somewhere between Predzellmoo and I. Its extended arm now limp on the surface of the water must have been her target. And then I realize that once again, Kitsune saved my life.

That bothers me more than I feel comfortable with.

We're always looking out for each other, but we don't even know one another. I can't tell for certain if we protect each other because we're ultimately good people and we don't want anyone getting hurt, or if it's something more than that – like the connection I feel when she's there.

Predzellmoo once again recollects itself and prepares for another attack. On me. Not on Kitsune. It's like she's not there and I'm the prime mark. For once, I don't feel the paralyzing fear of losing my life, or the anxiety worming around in my gut controlling my rational thought.

Come get it, I think.

Then something distracts me. A rumble of the ground has us all looking around for danger. Even Predzellmoo seems surprised. It's like a big jolt – strong and immediate. But it doesn't last longer than a few seconds.

And nothing happens. No danger. No creatures.

Up until Predzellmoo decides to attack when we're all distracted. It reaches for Kitsune's arm and pulls her under the water, face first.

This shocks me.

Predzellmoo hasn't attacked Kitsune since it arrived. At least, the creature hasn't tried to *really* kill her. And now it's holding her under water.

Intuitively, I summon another fireball, and this time, I throw it at Predzellmoo like I was throwing a baseball – with speed and force. The monster blows up into millions of tiny pieces of mud. I figure it'll come back, so I wait and watch the pieces on the surface of the water. They're unmoving, still, and unthreatening.

I start to think that maybe I finished it. But I know that's wishful thinking, even if earlier I vowed never to let it get away again. As we've been fighting, I get that it will be a lot harder than that.

At least tonight, it won't be back.

I look over at Kitsune. She's still under water. She's no longer beating the water as much as before. I presume she's running out of air now.

But why was she still under water if Predzellmoo was gone? There's nothing holding her there. I approach carefully and inspect Kitsune's position.

A large (and probably) heavy piece of mud-like material from Predzellmoo's body is placed between her shoulder blades. Essentially, that's most likely the only thing holding her beneath the surface.

I'm sure if she just realizes that nothing is restraining her, she could get up. I could just leave her there…

I sigh and roll my eyes at myself. This is stupid.

I push away the mud on Kitsune's back with my foot.

"Get up," I tell her, loud enough for Kitsune to hear me under water.

Kitsune rises before me, coughing and angrily filling her lungs with air.

"What happened?" she chokes loudly.

At least, it sounded really loud. Probably because the water stopped gushing from the ground and the wind died down finally. The storm passed – physically and metaphorically.

"What do you *think* happened?" I snap, irritated.

"Did you kill him for good?" she asks me, taking only a moment to examine the scene.

"No," I retort. "I don't think so." Even though it's hard to believe that blowing Predzellmoo into millions of pieces isn't enough to kill it, I'm sure that it's going to return eventually. It's just a feeling.

I peer around me to make absolutely sure it's gone. There's no sign that Predzellmoo intends to materialize.

"Thanks for saving me," Kitsune says to me, squeezing the excess water from her hair.

I know she's walking over to me because of the swooshing sound of the water around her legs coming closer. But I don't look at her. She undoubtedly doesn't know that I wasn't going to help her. That I was going to leave her there.

"You saved my life before. Now we're even," I respond, half hoping she doesn't hear a bit of the resentment there.

"You saved me to get even with me?" Kitsune questions.

I don't even have to look at her and I can tell she said that with an eyebrow raised, or with an unimpressed look on her face.

Her tone gives me the impression that she understands that I didn't save her life because she was in danger, but because I had to. A sense of duty, I suppose. But come on, she could have gotten up by herself. After all, she was able to get back up when her neck was broken. This was just a bit of mud.

I decide to be honest. "Yeah. I was going to let you drown."

I start to walk out of the crater and back on the surface of the street where the water now resides.

"You're lying," Kitsune replies. I can hear the smile on her face. She's not taking me seriously.

"There's always a bit of truth in every lie," I tell her, and shoot off into the night sky.

KASSIDY

18

BROKEN-HEARTED

I hope Dragoon is alright. After the fight at Halloween, I haven't seen her around. I thought I'd see her on patrol in the streets or feel her aura at some point between then and now. But nothing.

I think the explosion of that house hit her hard. The same way it did when she saw the dead teenagers at the convention centre. I feel bad for her.

And at the same time, I feel like it should have hit me harder than it has. I don't know what it is, but maybe I can compartmentalize my emotions better. And the fact that I'm not sure about it is a bit worrisome.

Am I rationalizing death?

Why can I do *that*, but I can't rationalize what I feel about Dana and Brydhen?

It's Monday morning and I dread getting out of bed for that very reason. Also, there's no point to it. It's the last day of school before Christmas break; I really don't see why they'd torture us into beginning a new week and then dismissing us for two weeks. It really doesn't make any sense to me. Yes, that's the part that makes the least sense – not the part where we still have to go to school despite multiple attacks in the city.

But there's something even worse about today: I'm afraid of talking to Dana. She spent the weekend over at Brydhen's place. I don't know what they did, and even if I tell myself that I don't care, I really *really* do care. Dana is going to tell me something I desperately wish not to hear. But I know it's inevitable. So, I turn my thoughts to something equally disturbing.

Predzellmoo loves me.

Technically, he loves Kitsune, *fox girl*. I know that Dragoon wasn't able to finish him off for good, so I know that he's going to come back claiming his undying love to me. The idea makes me shutter. The part that has me confused most is how a monster like that has a heart, let alone the ability to feel. What does *he* know about love?

When I get to school, the halls are deserted. For a moment, I wonder if school is out, until I see a few students, including Dana latched on to Brydhen's arm, Scotty, and Richard, all huddled together near the classrooms. As I get closer, their voices drop to mere whispers.

I feel ashamed and a little stressed. The selfish teenager inside me is furious at them for keeping something from me while the insecure teenager inside me feels like it's because of something I did. Why else would they whisper so that I don't hear them?

"What's going on?" I muster.

"Don't be too loud," Scotty warns me in a hushed tone, signaling something behind me with his eyes.

I peer over my shoulder at the hall supervisor. Mr. Pasa stands still, his glare fixed on our group. He almost looks possessed, especially with the shadows under his eyes and the reflection of the UV lights on his glasses. His hands are latched on the bottom of his blue and green cardigan, almost like he was trying to hold something back.

It dawns on me that the whispers weren't about me; Mr. Pasa must have followed me, and that's why the gang started whispering. I feel embarrassed for thinking that it was about me. Sometimes, I think that I'm so mature and responsible, being a superhero and earth's saviour and all, but other times, I'm so stupid and such a teenager. I forget the person I am and think too much about the person I'm supposed to be, or the hope I'm supposed to become. I don't realize that I'm still just a kid trying to grow up.

And I don't have time to grow up. I have to be a hero. I have to be strong. And I have to be everything people expect of me. There's so little time to be anything else.

"Did you hear what they said on the radio this morning?" Richard says under his breath as he moves us closer down the classroom corridor and out of Mr. Pasa's surveillance grid.

"Apparently, there's a city-wide curfew. It's too dangerous to stay out at night, especially after Halloween night. A lot of students are leaving, and they're not coming back," Richard informs us.

It's about time, I think.

I look at Dana. Where I thought I would see sadness, I see nothing but cold emptiness. She peers into my eyes and speaks calmly.

"They're closing down the school for good today," she says, and pulls her long sleeves further down to her fingers.

I knew it was going to happen eventually, but now I realize I won't be able to see my friends at all. I'll need a really good reason to leave the house to see them.

The bell rings and we all move forward. I'm about to return to get my books from the locker when Dana stops me. She winces and holds her wrist.

"What's wrong with your hand?" I ask, reaching out to pull up her sleeve.

Dana jerks away quickly and readjusts her sleeve. "Nothing," she answers. "Just been bothering me. But it's nothing."

I raise an eyebrow to tell her I'm not really buying it, but I'll let it go.

"We don't really have class today. All the students who did show up are confined to the cafeteria. Some teachers are bringing us some stuff to do. We don't know what it is yet," Dana says plainly.

"I hope they're not Christmas cards," I retort jokingly.

I expected at least a smile on Dana's lips, but my comment generated no effect at all. Dana is completely unresponsive.

She apologizes. "I'm just not feeling it today," she explains, looking away.

I frown. This isn't like her. What happened to her over the weekend with Brydhen that has got her so indifferent? My stare must have sent question marks her way because she takes me aside into one of the empty classrooms and closes the door behind us.

"What's going on?" I ask, curiosity building inside me.

"My parents are thinking of getting out of the city," she tells me.

And it's the first emotion I get to see from her. Sadness.

"Why?" is the only word I think to say. I'm really confused. And yet, it totally makes sense to leave the city.

"Because Kass, it's dangerous in the city these days. You never know when there's going to be an attack," Dana explains.

I know that already. But it never occurred to me that one of my friends could disappear from my life.

"It's just that …" she continues. Her eyes shift, like she's uncomfortable. Maybe concerned?

I wait for the end of the sentence, and I hate the suspense. Unless it's the announcement I dread hearing. But, of course it would be. Despite my utter disappointment, I stay silent. In my head, I vow to hide how it's making me feel. Dana doesn't need to know that. I'm sure I can try to be happy for them.

"It's Brydhen and I," Dana tells me.

And as Dana's mouth keeps moving, my heart sinks just knowing the words passing through her lips.

Brydhen has a girlfriend.

Dana is his girlfriend.

I can't tell if I'm more angry or broken-hearted. I repeat to myself that it doesn't affect me, and that I'll move on. I can be happy for them. But a storm of sequences flash in my mind in which I transform into Kitsune and Brydhen chooses me over Dana.

I choose to smile.

But really, I don't want to talk to her anymore. In fact, I don't want to see her at all. I feel like if she says another word, I'll punch her lights out.

I say to her instead: "Congratulations. I hope you're happy." I don't dare finish what's really in my head because it may not end well. But the words resound in my head, loud and traumatizing: *Because I'm not.* "We should go, though."

Dana nods in agreement and leads us through the door and down the hall.

"I'll be there in a minute," I say, as we walk past our locker.

Again, Dana nods and heads down to the cafeteria.

When she's well out of sight, I sigh. A spark suddenly explodes in me. I turn and punch right through our locker door. Then the spark disappears.

I peer around me, just to make sure no one saw. But there isn't anyone in the vicinity.

I pull my hand out, accidentally pulling the top of the locker door off its hinges as I do. My heart hurts – that irrational thumping that makes your chest burn, your stomach turn upside down – an uncomfortable feeling that makes you want to jump off a bridge, or in my case, fall to my knees and cry until my body goes dry (because I don't know if jumping off a bridge would damage me in any way).

I guess we never pick our sorrows.

My feet lead me back the way I came, through the entrance doors and out in the cold of a late Fall morning. I keep thinking that I should have made my move before Dana ever did, but where would that have gotten me? There's no point of fighting with Dana over a boy, and there's certainly no point in competing with her. She's obviously more beautiful than me, and her stamina more poignant. I would never come close to parallel; I would never be able to stand on such a pedestal.

The only pedestal I'm currently on is Predzellmoo's. I can't get the boy I love, but I can get the affections of an evil monster. I don't know if it's something I did, and I deserve this freak show, or if I'm just not good enough to be loved by Brydhen. Just the thought that I will never be a Dana for Brydhen breaks me even more. I feel like if I start to cry, I won't be able to stop.

A part of me wants to believe it's Dana's fault. After all, if she wasn't hogging the spotlight so much, I might have stood a chance with Brydhen. Didn't she know that Scotty was also very attracted to her, the same way she was to Brydhen, and that I was to Brydhen, and that Richard was to me?

I step out of my reverie for a moment and realize I'm walking home. People are wearing thick coats and gloves, while I'm carrying my coat and backpack in my hand. I don't even feel the cold because I'm so hot with anger.

I hate the couple holding on to each other at the corner store. I hate the man who's helping the old lady cross the street. I hate everything.

I feel like the world is still spinning, but I'm not spinning with it.

I turn onto the bike path and find myself completely alone. The bike path is surrounded in woods, secluded from the city's eyes. I feel like I can finally breathe here, like tranquility is in the wind itself.

I need air.

I look up and down the bike path to make sure no one is coming. I leave my bag and coat in the shadow of a tree, and I jump up, soaring into the clouds. When my chest finally feels the strength to pump freely, my eyes fill with water, and I can't stop the tears from falling. I let go of everything and cry and scream because I'm so devastated. The clouds imitate my feelings and turn dark and angry.

Sometime later, when the pain is finally gone from my heart, all that's left, is rushing anger. But this time, it's not directed at anyone in particular. Maybe just myself. I'm angry that I couldn't measure up to Brydhen's view of who his girlfriend should be. And I hate that my rational mind is telling me to let go, that things happen for a reason, or that high school drama never lasts. It's true. And I know it. But anger feels more real.

I slowly return to the ground where I left my bag and coat. They're drenched; in fact, the trees and the pavement are all soaked as if it rained. And maybe I made the sky cry with me. It doesn't sound too improbable, seeing as I have the power to manipulate water at my will.

I continue down the bike path, feeling released from heavy emotions, until I come to the next crossroads. There, the exterior market stretches out until downtown. But this late in the season, most markets have closed up shop for the winter. Or maybe they closed because it's too dangerous now. Some restaurants are still open, and the smell of a warm meal makes my stomach grumble and crave for a taste.

I enter the nearest restaurant, a cute Italian fast food place. I inhale the smell of strong spices and well-cooked meat. Decidedly, I'm going to satisfy my stomach here.

There are three men sitting in the dining area: an elderly man reading the newspaper, having the tiniest coffee and a warm carrot muffin with butter. A man in his mid-thirties, clean suit and black trench coat, fashion haircut, laptop set in front of him, is too busy to look up. And lastly, the young man at the counter eyes me idly. He's most likely my age, by the looks of him. He's tall, blond, short beard, and he wears a white, winter coat with navy blue, cargo pants.

I set my bag and coat on a chair and turn to the menu. The young woman behind the counter stares at me. She's either impatient or unimpressed that I'm taking my sweet time. She must be used to people knowing what they want. But I know what I want, and I know I can't have him.

A loud high-pitch scream distracts everyone - even the young gentleman at his laptop. And then more screams rip the air. People are running madly on the street, all heading in one direction like death was chasing after them.

Everyone in the restaurant is now standing, watching the world outside. And for a moment, the screaming stops, just long enough for a rumbling, like anger in a dog's throat, to shake the window glass of the restaurant.

I gigantic human hand moves into view, followed by an even bigger manly torso. I can't see the head, but upon seeing that it's levitating, I'm not expecting a human face. The bottom of the torso looks ripped from the rest of its body. The skin appears to be stretched, which would explain why some skin strands are dragging on the street. But there's no loss of blood, which tells me it's either been a long time since this creature lost its legs, or it's always been this way.

"All of you, stay here," I say out loud, over the screams of people on the street.

"What did you say, little girl?" the old man asks me. He stares me down, like he's trying to decide just why a girl my size has any business telling men what to do. His stare intensifies, like I should know my place.

"You're safer here," I tell him matter-of-factly, ignoring the older man's ignorance.

"Are you going out there?" the man in front of his laptop asks me. He sounds more confused than worried.

"Here we go," I whisper.

My golden rings appear instantaneously and disappear just as quickly, leaving me transformed into Kitsune. As I cross the threshold of the doorframe, I'm ready for a good fight. Unfortunately to this creature, he didn't pick the right day to makes its terrifying debut in the city. I have a lot of anger to take out on something, and this creature is going to be that something.

19

ANGER

I walk right in front of the creature. I stand my ground as I watch it approach. Its face is disfigured. It's hard to see any eyes or nose or mouth. It's mostly a mess of scars, wrinkles and dimples. It has no ears either. The only discernable feature about it is its exceedingly long, dark hair at the top of his head.

The creature is not bothered by my presence. In fact, it's just about to toss me out of the way with one swift movement of its arm. I raise my hand to catch its arm, but something else blocks the attack.

I think it's an invisible shield, but I know better.

If it was an invisible shield, I would have used it a long time ago for many other fights.

No, it's something else. It's like the air pushed back the enemy's arm.

So, I try the same maneuver when the creature tries to toss me again using its other arm. I raise my right hand, and the creature's attack is blocked for a second time. And now I know for sure that I'm capable of calling upon the wind, or the air, to my advantage. The air reacted with me, followed my movement, and allowed me to shield off attacks.

The creature growls again, the same way it had earlier in front of the restaurant. It sounds like a deep rumble, a canine's way of threatening. And this time, the creature raises both its arms above its head to squash me on the pavement street.

I feel bad for the creature. But just a little. It hasn't hurt anyone yet from what I can tell, but I can't take the chance that it could do some damage, like Predzellmoo. To be sure, this creature can't survive the next five minutes.

Before the creature has a chance to gather strength to pound on me, I push my palms forward as if to push away. And that's exactly what happens. The air rejects the creature and it's launched back into the woods near the bike path.

I whirl behind the creature and surprise it by latching on to its long hair. I push off the ground suddenly and when I feel like I'm high enough above the city, I spin the creature in circles. I spin faster and faster until I see the lone piece of skin that grew hair beginning to rip from the creature's skull.

I release the monster and watch as it goes twisting and turning in the air and finally, crashes into an abandoned storage unit.

I laugh bitterly.

"Goodbye," I mutter. Raising my palm for the last time, I expect to launch another air-like attack toward the building, one strong enough to pulverize it. But that's not what comes.

Instead, a heating ball materializes in my palm. It's the kind of heat that tickles at your skin when you're really cold, or like dipping into a warm bath. It's soothing. And yet, from the neon-blue colour of its heart, I presume this fireball is much hotter than it feels.

Just as I'm about to push the fireball forward, another blast of fire comes from below. The abandoned storage unit explodes and showers the surrounding area with debris.

I close my hand and find the source of the attack.

Dragoon is staring at me from the ground. It's nothing against her, but I don't feel like being bothered at the moment – especially not from my supposed *partner* who almost let me die last time we saw one another.

I turn away and fly as quickly as I can from the scene.

"Where are you going?" Dragoon's voice reaches me from not far behind.

"Where you can leave me alone," I retort impatiently.

Dragoon laughs. "What makes you think I'll leave you alone, *partner*?"

I halt my flight impulsively. Dragoon moves around me to see my visage. But I really don't want to look into hers. The last time we fought together, she was cold and murderous. She could have let me die, and she chose to save me only to get even with me. If that's how the earth's saviour thinks, there won't be many people left alive to save in four years from now.

"Get away from me," I spit.

"I'm just trying to figure you out, that's all," Dragoon says, with the same tone that always makes me feel like I'm so stupid.

"What's wrong with you?" I ask, giving in to my frustration and exasperation.

"What's wrong with *you*?" Dragoon redirects the question to me. "You look depressed. And you took care of a monster all on your own when yesterday you were *drowning* for my help."

Dragoon snorts slightly.

"Shut up! You're not funny!" I shoot back at her, so annoyed with her.

A powerful gust of wind rips at Dragoon's skin on her arms and her stomach. Dragoon's inconspicuous smile fades. Her features evolve to equal what I feel inside. Her mouth is open, gasping for air.

For a second, I feel bad.

For a second, I'm tempted to apologize. She didn't deserve that.

Dragoon looks at the wounds I caused. The slashes on her arms and on her stomach heal almost instantaneously. She straightens, and I can feel a surge of energy from her. But she doesn't show it.

Dragoon's revenge is immediate and expected. A whip of fire springs from her fist and lacerates my hand.

My entire body shakes violently. But as I look at the damage on my hand, it's already barely noticeable. I take a deep breath. I'm not even angry anymore. I'm just tired.

"You're pathetic," are the only words I muster before I fly away.

In my back yard, I return my appearance to Kassidy. I walk inside.

No one is here.

And I guess that's best for everyone, because I really don't know what I'll do if my dad or my sister anger me even more.

I storm into my room and lay in my bed until sleep comes.

20

TRUTH BE TOLD

(T minus 1420 days until End)

I wake up in my bed close to mid-afternoon. I'm still in yesterday's clothes, and my shoes are still on. As I sit up, I feel like my head is about to explode. It's thumping so heavily like I've never felt before. My sister's loud music reaches my ears and I wish the world had stayed silent like a moment ago.

I stretch my limbs and kick off my shoes. If my dad ever found out I stepped inside the house with my shoes on, I'd be in deep trouble. I just hope he doesn't find out that I slept in for so long. So, I grab a change of clothes and head downstairs for a warm shower.

My sister, sitting at the computer, spins the chair around and stares at me like I'm absolutcly disgusting. "Welcome back to life," she tells me.

I don't respond as I walk past her and lock myself in the bathroom. The quiet and the rush of water on my skin is exactly what I need. I try my best to avoid thinking of Dana and Brydhen, and instead concentrate on the calm that the water brings me. I trace the length of the scar on my arm and recognize that it's the still the same size as before even though it's been months since my first fight with Predzellmoo where I got this lovely present. This *very* permanent present.

I don't take too much time in the shower because I feel like I have to keep busy, and in the same way, keep my mind off things that hurt. I get dressed quickly and return to my bedroom.

"Hey," my sister calls from the doorway.

"What do you want?" I ask shortly.

"What the heck is wrong with you today?" she snaps back at me, matching my mood.

"What do you want?" I repeat with more patience.

My sister growls resentfully. "Dana called. She said it was an emergency – super important." And then she walks away.

Surely, she went back downstairs to her annoying music. Within seconds, the loud thumping of a base shakes the walls.

Just as I thought.

I want to call Dana back and find out what's so important, but I really don't want to talk to her. She probably wants to hang out and that's the last thing I want to do with her today. Especially after what happened yesterday, I really don't want to see anyone.

But curiosity gets the better of me. She *did* tell me she might be getting out of town. Even though I'm angry with her – borderline jealous – I still don't want her to leave me. So, I pick up the phone and dial Dana's number. I want to know what's so important.

Dana picks up the phone and says she has something important to tell me. She sounds extremely nervous. "Come on over," I offer.

When Dana arrives, she looks just as nervous as she sounded over the phone. I invite her in and lead her over to my bedroom for privacy and some quiet from my sister's loud music.

"What's wrong? What's going on?" I ask softly, not wanting to put on too much pressure.

"Why did you leave yesterday?" she replies as she sits down on the edge of my bed.

"I got a headache. I didn't want to stay at school if there weren't any classes," I lie with ease. "What did they have you do, anyways?"

"Christmas cards," Dana says, but I know it's a comical lie meant to ease the tension.

I giggle but press on.

Dana shrugs. "They just told us to go home and then they closed the school permanently."

"Oh," I say in response. "So you didn't stay at school long either, then."

"No," Dana confirms. "Good thing, too. 'Cuz this monster thing was around the market after it left the school."

"And Kitsune stopped it in time," I say.

Dana nods slowly, almost suspiciously. "How do you know?"

"Saw it on the news," I answer quickly.

"Did the news also mention what the monster did to our school?" Dana adds but doesn't wait for my answer. "Our school is gone – went up in flames. Lucky it was already evacuated."

I must look stupid with my eyebrows raised and my mouth slightly open. "Oh my god," I murmur.

Dana takes in a deep breath and continues. "There are so many attacks on the student population, and now the school is gone," she sighs. "It doesn't make sense to me, though. It's not strategic to destroy the school if that's where all the students reunite," Dana ponders out loud. "Especially if the target is the students."

"But if you think about it, there was never an attack on the school until now," I correct. "The school must have acted as a kind of untouchable refuge or something like that. And now that the school officially announced to close its doors …" I leave the thought in the air.

"A refuge?" Dana repeats. "For who? The bad guys?"

"Yeah, the bad guys – whatever's attacking us," I agree. And as I say it out loud, it occurs to me that I might not be so far off the reservation. But that would also mean that the witch was also at school, making it *her* refuge.

"I guess that makes sense," Dana thinks, but she's lost in thought, considering my conclusion.

Dana's eyes suddenly lock on my bedside table. She frowns, the same way she usually does when she doesn't understand something. I follow her glare and find the object of her attention. I swallow my idiocy. There, in plain sight, is the thorn I pulled out of Dragoon's spine – the thing that rendered Dragoon as weak as a human.

I try to reach forward to hide the object, but Dana is quicker. She snatches it from my bedside table and examines it closely.

"Where did you get this?" she interrogates, her breathing quickening.

And for the first time, I can't think of a lie. The images of that day replay in my mind: Dragoon's dying body reposing in my arms, her weight on me, her vitality slowly dissipating.

"Where did you get this?" Dana repeats. This time, she's insistent, holding the thorn between us, her eyes accusatory.

My mind struggles to find something to say, *anything* to say! But all I hear is the thumping of my heart in my chest. Before I know it, Dana grips my shoulders. She's strong and she holds me steady.

There's nothing I can do even if I wanted to.

"Kass, tell me the truth. Where did you get this?"

Then all my thoughts clear.

"How …" I start in utter acknowledgement. "… do you know what it is?"

Dana quickly, and even faster than I can see, rips my sleeve. Upon seeing the scar on my arm, Dana releases her grip on me, her hands still in mid-air. She's staring at the scarred gash on my arm: the wound I was inflicted during my first fight with Predzellmoo.

My body never healed from that.

And if Dana knows about the thorn, and my scar, then she must be…

While I still have the chance, I clasp Dana's hand and pull up the sleeve of her sweater. Her hand reveals something I half expected: a purple scar, caused by the spider venom that cut through Dragoon's skin.

"Dragoon! You're Dragoon!" I muster in a breath.

"And you're Kitsune!"

From the same author, discover "The Dragon Warriors" series!

Manufactured by Amazon.ca
Bolton, ON